"You've found the courage to dine with the devil.

"Let's see if you have the courage to let him kiss you," Julian whispered, his mouth hovering above hers.

My God, Emelina thought bleakly, what is it about this man? Before she could summon the protest she knew she ought to make, she became aware of the heat of his fingers alongside her cheek and then the far more intimate heat of his mouth.

How could a kiss be at once marauding and persuasive? Demanding, yet coaxing? How could a man like this kiss a woman as if she were an infinitely valuable and precious creature? Where Emelina expected rough aggression, she received sensual insistence. Where she expected dominance, she received warm inducement.

She closed her eyes, not daring to move as his lips teased hers. Then, with a soft little moan, she succumbed to the sensual demand....

STEPHANIE JAMES

is a pseudonym for bestselling, award-winning author **Jayne Ann Krentz**. Under various pseudonyms—including Jayne Castle and Amanda Quick—Ms. Krentz has over twenty-two million copies of her books in print. Her fans admire her versatility as she switches between historical, contemporary and futuristic romances. She attributes a "lifelong addiction to romantic daydreaming" as the chief influence on her writing. With her husband, Frank, she currently resides in the Pacific Northwest.

Jayne Ann Krentz
writing as

Stephanie James

The Devil To Pay

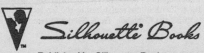

Silhouette® Books
Published by Silhouette Books
America's Publisher of Contemporary Romance

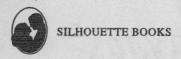

SILHOUETTE BOOKS

ISBN 0-373-80684-1

THE DEVIL TO PAY

This edition published by arrangement with Harlequin Books S.A.

Visit us at www.romance.net

Printed in U.S.A.

Available Titles From
STEPHANIE JAMES

A PASSIONATE BUSINESS
AFFAIR OF HONOR
BATTLE PRIZE
BODY GUARD
CAUTIOUS LOVER
CORPORATE AFFAIR
DANGEROUS MAGIC
FABULOUS BEAST
GAMBLER'S WOMAN
GAMEMASTER
GOLDEN GODDESS
GREEN FIRE
LOVER IN PURSUIT
NIGHT OF THE MAGICIAN
NIGHTWALKER
PRICE OF SURRENDER
RAVEN'S PREY
RECKLESS PASSION
RENAISSANCE MAN
SAXON'S LADY
SERPENT IN PARADISE
STORMY CHALLENGE
THE CHALLONER BRIDE
THE DEVIL TO PAY
THE SILVER SNARE
TO TAME THE HUNTER
VELVET TOUCH
WIZARD

For Suzanne,
a good friend on the same path.
WRITE ON!

One

She couldn't shake the feeling that she was being watched.

Emelina Stratton paused, her hand on the knob of the back door of the deserted beach house, and nervously swung the flashlight in an arc. It barely pierced the gathering fog. She had about ten feet of visibility, and even that would soon be gone. There was nothing to be seen in the writhing shadows that clung to the lonely stretch of beach.

It was only her all too-vivid imagination at work again, she told herself resolutely. Lively enough on an average day, her imagination was running wild under the present circumstances.

Getting a grip on herself, she tossed the long, heavy braid of chestnut hair back over one shoulder and tried the doorknob. Locked. Of course it would be locked. It had been too much to hope that Leighton would have been so careless as to leave the door conveniently open. She wiggled the knob fruitlessly for a few seconds and then gave up. It would have to be one of the windows. Would she dare to break one and pray that Leighton would assume it was only an act of vandalism by some young kids?

The sensation of being under observation returned again as Emelina started down the back steps. Once again she cast an uneasy glance around the dark, foggy beach. Several yards away a light surf lapped almost gently at the rocky Oregon shoreline. Above the soft sound of the waves she could hear nothing alarming. But the unconscious response of her body to impending danger grew stronger, lifting the delicate hairs on the nape of her neck and sending small shivers along each nerve ending.

Nothing moved in the surrounding shadows. Emelina rubbed her hands along her arms. It was cold here at midnight on the Oregon coast. The close-fitting black sweater she had worn wasn't nearly enough protection from the bite of the fog-shrouded air. Pity. It had looked exactly right for a commando mission.

Damn her imagination! It was a poor companion on a job like this. Perhaps professional burglars got along in their chosen profession precisely because they lacked the ability to dream up such vivid images of disaster! Emelina couldn't believe that anyone would attempt this sort of thing on a regular basis if he or she had to put up with all these nerve-wracking imaginings!

As she tested the window frame she told herself for the hundredth time that there was very little likelihood of anyone else's being around this quiet strip of beach at this hour. The fog was thickening by the minute, which should deter the average midnight stroller, even if there were any such living in the quiet little coastal village nearby. There were a couple of other houses behind Leighton's, all deserted at this time of year. There were also a few cottages up on the bluff overlooking the beach. They were inhabited. In fact, Emelina was living in one of them, herself, but as far as she could tell, everyone else was in bed for the night. "Early to bed, early to rise" seemed to be a local motto. They rolled the streets up early in town.

The window didn't budge an inch.

"Damn!"

With the short exclamation of disgust, Emelina stepped back and swung around to search for a likely looking rock. She went utterly still at sight of the pair who had materialized out of the fog behind her.

"Oh, my God!" The words were a whisper of sound as she sucked in a sharp, frightened breath. Instinctively her startled gaze went first to the Doberman before shifting to its master.

The sleek black-and-tan dog didn't move. It sat quietly on its haunches, watching her intently. The small, sensitive ears were pricked alertly, and the unhuman, dark gaze never wavered.

Slowly, unwillingly, Emelina lifted her eyes to the dark, dangerous man who stood beside the dog. It struck Emelina in that moment that Julian Colter was as quietly lethal looking as his Doberman. It was the first time she had seen either of them at this range however, and up close the flashlight's beam revealed that the man radiated a more subtle element of menace than the beast. For in addition to the somehow graceful threat of power he seemed to share with the dog, Julian Colter wore an aura of command. He was clearly master of both the Doberman and himself.

"Good evening." The soft, gravelly voice drew Emelina's nerves taut. She felt as if she had just stepped into a Dracula film and was being introduced to the count, himself. "If you're looking for a place to spend the night, I can offer far better accommodations than you'll find in that deserted house."

I'll bet, Emelina thought grimly. Could she outrun him? She swallowed with difficulty. Even if that were a possibility, and she sincerely doubted it, common sense warned her that no one could outrun the Doberman. Did Colter recognize her? Had he seen her occasionally from a distance just as she'd seen him during the past week? What the hell was he doing down here on this beach at this hour?

"No." Emelina chewed on her very dry lower lip and tried again, jamming her free hand into the front pocket of her black denim jeans in an effort to hide the fact that it was trembling. "No, I wasn't looking for a place to sleep." Had he mistaken her for a passing hitchhiker looking for a convenient bed for the night? Good. Maybe he hadn't recognized her. "I... I was just out for a walk."

"A walk." Julian Colter took a pace closer, ignoring the flashlight's glare. The Doberman followed. The gathering fog swirled around them both. "It's a rather unusual hour for a walk, isn't it?" he inquired with grave politeness.

In the harsh glow of the light she held in her hand Emelina could barely make out his features. But she could see enough to tell that his gaze was almost totally unreadable. "You seem to be out doing the same thing," she pointed out with bravado.

"Ah, yes," he agreed with a faint, very polite inclination of his head. A brief flash of white betrayed the smallest of amused smiles. "But, then, I have a reason to be out here on the beach at midnight."

"You...you do?" Emelina gnawed on her lip. Had she unwittingly interrupted a dangerous rendezvous?

"Ummm. I was following you."

"What?" For an instant sheer outrage combined with Emelina's fear. "*Following* me! You had no right to do that! Following me! Whatever for?"

"Well, there isn't a whole lot to do in this village, as you may or may not have noticed," he murmured with mild apology. "You interest me."

"Good God! I'm not hanging around this godforsaken place for the sole purpose of providing you with a little entertainment!"

"I realize that. Which brings up the intriguing question of what you are doing around this place, doesn't it? Why don't you come back to the cottage with Xerxes and me and we'll talk about that little matter over a glass of brandy. It's getting chilly down here, don't you think?"

The dog got to his feet at the sound of his name and glanced up expectantly at his master. Emelina stared at both of them and thought again about running. "No," she whispered. "That's impossible. I have no wish to go to your place with you, Mr. Colter!"

The shark's smile came and went again. "I see you know my name. That gives you something of an advantage, I'm afraid. I don't know yours."

"Good," Emelina retorted unthinkingly.

He appeared mildly regretful. "Come along, night lady. I feel in the need of a few answers before I go to sleep."

He took a step closer and Emelina lost her nerve completely. In blind panic she turned and fled back along the beach. It was not the smartest move she could have made. The shoreline was rocky and uneven, and with the swirling fog she could barely see five feet in front of her.

But she ran, recklessly, heedlessly, as if Dracula and his pet werewolf were on her heels. Emelina didn't see any other choice in that moment except flight. She knew what the townspeople were saying about Julian Colter, and memory of their low-voiced speculation was more than enough to send her fleeing.

The werewolf caught up with her first. There had been no shouted warnings to stop, no sharp, menacing bark. Neither man nor beast had wasted time and effort on such deterrents. They had both pursued silently, having no intention of allowing her to escape.

The Doberman appeared out of the fog at Emelina's side, running easily, his mouth open and laughing in the fitful moonlight. Emelina swung around and braced herself for the attack, her hands in front of her.

But the dog didn't attack. He came to a halt, too, sitting on his haunches and smiling up at her. Belatedly, Emelina realized that he thought it was all a game. He hadn't been ordered to attack. The Doberman had simply followed when she'd started running, enjoying the night race.

She was staring at the animal when its owner stepped out of the mist. If Julian Colter had been running, there was no evidence to document the fact. Even as Emelina dragged in a harsh breath she realized that the man looked no more strained than the dog.

"If you take him running like that very often, you'll have a friend for life." Colter smiled, indicating the Doberman. "He loves a good race." Then, before she could prepare herself, he reached out and took hold of Emelina's arm. "But it's not really a good night for running, is it? Let's go back to the cottage. Come on, Xerxes," he added, glancing down at the dog.

Emelina found herself going along as obediently, if not as willingly, as Xerxes. There really wasn't much choice. Strong fingers were locked around her upper arm now, not yet painful but full of the promise of unshakable will. Julian Colter was after some answers tonight, and now nothing was going to stand in his way.

Desperately Emelina tried to marshal her thoughts. She had to come up with a convincing tale or she was only going to dig the grave deeper than ever. Grave. What a horrible image. She gritted her teeth and cursed her own imagination again.

"Do you have a name, night lady?"

There was no point lying about it, she supposed.

"Emelina. Emelina Stratton." The words came out sullenly, masking the fear she felt.

"Emelina. I like that. I'll call you Emmy. You don't have to be afraid of me, Emmy," he added surprisingly.

"I'm not. At least, no more than I would be afraid of any man who accosted me on the beach at midnight!" she exclaimed with a great depth of feeling.

Colter nodded understandingly as he guided her up the path to the bluff overlooking the beach. "I only want a few answers, Emmy."

"Why? What business is it of yours what I do at midnight?"

"I told you, you interest me. You arrive a week ago, all alone, and take a cottage that's not more than a short block from my own. It's the middle of winter, which is not a popular time for tourists in this part of the country. You spend your days keeping watch on that deserted beach house and then one night I see you making your way down the street toward the beach path. I find you about to commit an act of breaking and entering at midnight. I ask myself what anyone would hope to find worth stealing in that old place and I ask myself why a woman like you would come here in the middle of winter to carry out such an act. And I can't seem to come up with any answers. So Xerxes and I decided we'd just follow along tonight and ask you. Simple, hmmm?"

"Too simple. This is none of your business, Mr. Colter, I guarantee it. It has nothing whatsoever to do with you." Emelina shuddered as she thought about what she had overheard concerning this man.

Mafia, the waitress in the cafe had confided to the diner in the next booth only that morning as Emelina had sipped coffee. *Probably hiding out while things cool down back east.*

The waitress, Emelina knew, was not alone in her analysis. *Syndicate type,* the clerk at the grocery store had decided when the person in the checkout line ahead of Emelina had mentioned Colter's name. A high-level Mob boss who had found it convenient to take a winter vacation on the Oregon coast.

Whatever the truth, there was no doubt Julian Colter had managed to incite a great deal of speculation among the villagers. He kept to himself, was chillingly polite when he found it necessary to deal with a clerk or a salesperson in town, and went everywhere with the Doberman. Everyone knew Dobermans were savage beasts, trained for attack and bred for ferocity. As far as the townspeople were concerned, the dog was a fitting companion for the man.

Emelina risked a slanting, sideways glance at the man who walked by her side, holding her captive. It was true. There were certain similarities between man and dog. She shivered. She'd only seen Julian Colter from a distance until tonight. Now, the impression the villagers had formed was easy to understand. Emelina saw nothing to make her doubt their conclusions about his profession.

There was a harsh ruthlessness in the unhandsome profile. The hawklike nose and aggressive jawline were etched with power. The damp air had left the pelt of coal black hair looking darker than ever in the mist-refracted moonlight. There was iron at the temples, a gray that would be spreading more quickly through the black hair as the man neared forty.

Forty probably wasn't far off for him, Emelina decided uncharitably. If forced to name his age, she would have said thirty-eight or thirty-nine. She would also have said that, in terms of experience, Julian Colter was probably a good deal older. Judging by the grimly hewn lines at the edges of his mouth and the detached, cynical expression in his dark eyes, Colter had gained his experience the rough way.

The rest of him was hard and lean, but beneath the dark trousers and heavy leather jacket he wore, his body moved with a masculine grace that seemed to echo the dog's. Lethal, yet somehow beautiful in its own fashion. Emelina gnawed worriedly on her lip as they started up the path to the top of the bluff. Was he carrying a gun under that leather jacket? What was her best course of action now? Somehow she had to convince him that she was no threat to him.

For that could be the only reason he had bothered to follow her tonight, she decided with sudden inspiration. A Mafia chieftain who was hiding out under an assumed name in a lonely coastal fishing village would naturally be suspicious of another stranger in town. Yes, that was the explanation for Julian Colter's interest in her. Almost idly she found herself wondering what his real name was and then promptly decided that it was best if she didn't find out.

Xerxes bounded ahead to the top of the cliff and stopped to wait for the two humans. When they finally arrived he turned and trotted toward the nearest weathered cottage. He waited again on the doorstep as Julian silently dug out his keys and fitted them into the lock.

"Probably no need to lock one's doors around this neighborhood, but some habits are hard to break, aren't they?" Julian drawled, shoving open the door for his unwilling guest. "Besides, with all these strangers roaming around at night..."

Xerxes delicately pushed his nose under Emelina's hand as if he were urging her inside. Emelina jumped at the sudden contact.

"It's all right. I think Xerxes likes you," Julian murmured, prodding her gently over the threshold.

"How can you tell?" she muttered resentfully, snatching her hand away from the dog's sleek head.

"Well, he hasn't torn your throat out yet, has he?"

Emelina stared at the brief grin Julian tossed in her direction as he switched on a light. "Your sense of humor leaves something to be desired," she told him with a shudder. Automatically she moved toward the remnants of a fire which still flickered warmly on the hearth across the room.

"Sorry. I don't get much chance to practice it. My sense of humor, I mean." He watched her as she nervously crossed the bare wooden floor. The cottage was typical of the weather-beaten houses that dotted the hills overlooking the ocean. Sparsely furnished with old throw rugs, overstuffed and somewhat tattered furniture, it had, nevertheless, a surprisingly pleasant atmosphere of crumbling comfort, especially with the fire blazing in the fireplace. "I'll get you a brandy. It's damn cold out there, and you aren't wearing anything other than a thin sweater."

Emelina said nothing. She could hardly explain that she'd been concerned with freedom of movement and hadn't wanted to be dragged down by a heavy jacket in case it was necessary to run or hide. She kept her narrowed, wary gaze on the fire as Julian moved about the small kitchen, pouring brandy. She was aware of his cool assessment.

She also was well aware of what he saw as his night-dark gaze roved over her. The long, chestnut braid hung down the center of her back, pulling the rich length of hair away from her face to reveal an ordinary set of features. At least, Emelina had always thought of them as ordinary. Large, faintly slanted hazel eyes that were neither blue nor green dominated the otherwise unimpressive line of a firm nose and a soft mouth. She was thirty-one years old.

Taken independently there was nothing remarkable about the individual features, but together they comprised an expressive, deeply individual face which reflected the personality of the woman behind the blue green eyes. No discerning person looking at Emelina would have doubted the underlying intelligence or the imaginative curiosity and awareness that were such strong elements of her nature. It was a face that could easily reflect laughter or dismay or any of a number of emotions. Those who knew her well were convinced that the hazel eyes sometimes changed color when those emotions were especially intense.

When she glanced in a mirror Emelina told herself there was a look of good health about her features. A look that was all too robustly repeated in the rounded curves of her very feminine frame. Emelina could have cheerfully done with a little less of that healthy appearance, she had often decided. The black denims fit rather snugly over a softly rounded derriere, and the black sweater outlined full breasts. She found herself wishing she'd worn a bra. But, then, she hadn't exactly expected to run into anyone else this evening!

"Feeling more comfortable?" Julian inquired politely as he returned to the living room and handed her a brandy. Xerxes had settled down on the small rug in front of the fireplace, sharing the warmth with Emelina.

"Yes, thank you." Reluctantly Emelina took a sip of the brandy and tried to think how one made casual conversation with a Mob boss. Somehow she must convince him that, whatever his business was here, hers was entirely unconnected!

"Sit down, Emmy." Julian sounded as if he were retasting her name. He indicated a fat, comfortable chair behind her. Emelina sank down into it slowly, wishing she could think of some alternative. He took the faded chair across from her and propped his feet up on the hassock. Across the rim of his brandy glass, his dark eyes met hers. "Now take your time and tell me why that old house interests you so."

"It has nothing to do with you," she assured him earnestly. At least there had been no gun visible when he'd removed the dark leather jacket, she thought in relief. "I couldn't sleep and just decided to go for an evening stroll."

"At midnight?" he inquired with gentle skepticism.

"I like to walk on the beach at midnight!"

"In nothing but a light sweater and jeans?"

"Mr. Colter, I don't know why you should be so interested in my nocturnal habits," she retorted a little desperately. "I give you my word they have absolutely nothing at all to do with you!"

"Perhaps that is a little matter which could be altered," he suggested easily.

"I beg your pardon?" Emelina stared at him, totally at a loss.

"That was a subtle masculine pass, Emmy," he explained dryly, mouth crooking with genuine amusement as he viewed her frown. "Apparently a little too subtle, since it seems to have gone straight over your head. I'm surprised at you. You look like a reasonably intelligent woman, and you're certainly old enough to recognize innuendoes, subtle or otherwise."

Emelina finally realized what he was saying and to her chagrin flushed a deep, rosy shade. "Believe me, Mr. Colter, I have no intention of combining my nocturnal habits with yours! I thought we were discussing something much more serious than...than whatever it is you're trying to discuss." She got to her feet, ignoring Xerxes, who lifted his head and watched her alertly. "If you went to the trouble of following me and dragging me back here just to suggest we spend the night together, you've wasted your time and that of your dog! I am not the least bit interested!"

"Because you're in town on business?"

"Exactly. Good night, Mr. Colter. I'll see myself home." Perhaps if she moved quickly enough she could outbluff him. Xerxes, however, reached the door ahead of her and sat in front of it looking extremely hopeful. It was enough to bring Emelina to a full stop. She didn't trust the Doberman any more than she trusted his master. That hopeful look was probably reflecting the dog's inner wish to have an excuse to go for her throat. Slowly she turned around to glare at Julian, who continued to sprawl in his chair.

For a moment silence hung in the room. None of the three moved. Julian was clearly not going to call off the dog. He simply sat quietly and sipped at the brandy, his eyes never leaving her. Xerxes waited behind her.

Helplessly, her mind full of vivid images of a Doberman's attack, Emelina drifted back to her chair and picked up her glass of brandy. It was becoming increasingly obvious that she wasn't going anywhere until Julian Colter had his answers. But if it was answers he wanted, why had he bothered with the small pass? It occurred to Emelina that if there was one thing more dangerous than a Mafia boss, it might be a bored Mafia boss on vacation.

"Would you like a little more brandy?" Julian finally inquired politely.

"No, thank you." Emelina sat stiffly in her chair and focused on the fire. She didn't like his quiet intimidation, but she didn't have the faintest idea of how to get out from under it. Unless simply telling the truth might do the trick. "Mr. Colter, this is all very complicated and it doesn't concern you."

"Julian," he corrected softly.

"Julian." Emelina's frown deepened. "If I tell you

why I was down on the beach tonight, will you call off your dog?''

Xerxes, as if sensing he was the subject of discussion, paced over to her chair and thrust his head into her lap. Emelina recoiled slightly.

''I don't think my dog wants to be called off,'' Julian observed pleasantly. ''He likes you.''

''Perhaps you'd better explain to him that I'm basically a cat person,'' Emelina suggested wryly as she hesitantly touched the animal's neck. Xerxes's ears twitched.

''Xerxes doesn't worry about the competition. He knows he can take what he wants.''

Emelina glanced up sharply. ''Are you trying to tell me that you and Xerxes share a similar philosophical approach to life?'' she challenged, somewhat surprised by her own dash of boldness.

''I simply made a statement about my dog, Emmy. Don't read too much into it.''

Emelina sighed, focusing on the problem she was facing. Unconsciously her fingers began to rub Xerxes behind the ears. ''That house on the beach belongs to someone I know, Julian.''

''Go on.''

''He's not a very nice person.'' Julian probably understood people like Eric Leighton, she realized. ''The man who owns it is blackmailing my brother.''

''Blackmailing your brother!'' His astonishment appeared genuine, and Emelina wondered briefly at it. Blackmail and related endeavors must be old hat to a man like this. ''Whatever it was I expected to hear, it wasn't that. Please go on with the tale, Emmy."

She shrugged, trying to appear casual about the whole thing. "There isn't much more to tell. I'm here to see if I can find out anything that will help my brother get Leighton off his back."

"Leighton presumably being the owner of that beach house?"

"That's right. Now if you don't mind..."

"Relax, Emmy," Julian advised gently. "You're not going anywhere just yet. You must realize you've opened a whole can of worms."

"None of this involves you!" she insisted. "Not unless...unless..." She broke off in sudden shock and swung her stricken eyes to his face.

"Unless I'm mixed up with Leighton? Is that what's worrying you now?"

She swallowed. "Leighton's always been a loner," she breathed. "I can't see him working for you or anyone else. I can see him having a partner, but I don't see *you* in that role."

Julian arched one black brow. "I can assure you he's not working for me."

Emelina sagged a little with relief. What a horrible mess that would have been! Dazed by the near miss, she sank back against the chair's cushion, her fingers still massaging the sensitive area behind Xerxes's ears. The dog shouldered a little closer and his eyes closed. A temporarily contented werewolf. "Well, that's really all there is to it. I'm hoping to find something useful around that house of his. Something my brother can use."

Julian eyed her consideringly. "Why isn't your brother the one keeping tabs on the house?"

"We don't want Leighton to become suspicious. My brother lives in Seattle. He works for a large corporation there. If he were simply to disappear for a few weeks to come down here and keep watch on the house, someone would be bound to notice and then Leighton might find out."

"And you, on the other hand, are free to disappear from your social milieu for several weeks?" he drawled. "There's no one back home wondering where the hell you've disappeared to?"

"Writers are expected to need time to themselves," Emelina told him proudly.

"You're a writer?"

"That's correct," she snapped.

He paused a moment and then asked carefully, "Have you written anything I might have had occasion to read?"

"I doubt it."

"What have you published?" Julian persisted.

"Well, I haven't actually been published yet," she confided in a little rush. "But I'm working on it. I have two manuscripts out to publishers right now, in fact! I'm trying to create a category that's a cross between romance fiction and science fiction."

"Is there, uh, much of a market for that sort of thing?" he asked delicately.

"No," Emelina admitted morosely.

"I see." There was a wealth of meaning behind the simple words, and Emelina ground her teeth a little savagely. She'd heard too many people say those particular words in exactly that manner. An unpublished writer was often the object of much pity, condescension and gentle scorn. One of these days, she vowed silently for the millionth time, things will be different.

"Is there anything else you'd care to know about this evening, Julian?" she inquired far too sweetly.

"Yes, as a matter of fact, I am curious about one other thing," he smiled. "Whose idea was it?"

"What idea?"

"The idea of coming down here to keep watch on that beach house?"

"Mine. Why?" she muttered.

The shark's smile broadened, and Julian's dark eyes flickered briefly with genuine amusement. "I just wondered."

"I get the feeling you're not taking all this too seriously, which is just fine with me," Emelina ground out emphatically. "May I please go home now?"

"If you don't mind, I do have one or two other questions."

Emelina closed her eyes in silent dismay. The overly polite words were tantamount to a command to stay where she was. "What else would you like to know?"

"If you're still awaiting discovery back in New York, how are you managing to eat in the meantime?"

Her eyes flew open. "Why in the world should that matter to you?"

"I am cursed with this insatiable curiosity where

you're concerned,'' he apologized humbly. ''As I keep pointing out to you, there simply isn't very much to interest me around this burg.''

''Well, don't think you're going to amuse yourself with me!''

He inclined his head in acknowledgment of the statement and then sat waiting with a patience that annoyed Emelina. Unable to resist the silent pressure, she answered him gruffly. ''I work in a bookstore in Portland.''

''Ah.''

''What's that supposed to mean? Ah?'' she demanded aggressively.

''It means, ah, you're not being supported by anyone while you hone your writing skills,'' he explained smoothly.

''Of course not! For heaven's sake! I'm thirty-one years old and quite capable of supporting myself. I have been doing so for a long time!'' she stated proudly.

''Not sinking further and further into debt while you live on the expectation of huge advances from the publishing world, hmmm?'' he teased lightly.

Emelina's eyes blazed with sudden fury. ''I am not in debt! I make it a point never to get into debt! I pay my bills, Mr. Colter. Every last one of them.''

He blinked lazily in response to her unexpected vehemence. It wasn't his fault, she realized belatedly. Julian Colter could hardly know about her own personal history, which included an irresponsible father who had left a mountain of debts behind when he'd been killed in a stock car crash and a handsome, graduate student husband who had left a huge pile of student loans and related bills to pay when he'd run off with a classmate. No one who didn't know her background could understand the importance to Emelina of being free of debt. She sighed inwardly, wishing she hadn't overreacted to the comment Julian had made.

"Okay," he said agreeably. "So you're a would-be writer who pays her bills. And it was your idea to come to the coast to keep an eye on this beach house. You claim your brother is being blackmailed...."

"He is!"

"And you're running around at midnight in the middle of winter looking for evidence to use against the blackmailer," Julian concluded. "Quite a tale, Emmy."

"You don't believe me?" she whispered. Her hand paused on Xerxes's neck, and the dog opened one eye reproachfully.

"The funny part is, I think I do." Julian smiled. "It's probably a little too crazy to be anything other than the truth."

Emelina let out her breath in relief. "In that case, I'd appreciate it if you'd let me go home now. As you can see, none of this has anything to do with you. It's just a coincidence that we happened to wind up on the same beach together, Julian," she ended deliberately in case he'd missed the point. "I really have no interest at all in whatever reason you have for being here in the same town."

"I'm crushed. No interest in me at all?"

Once more Emelina surged to her feet. Xerxes nudged her leg with his nose, protesting the change in position, but she ignored him. He didn't seem quite so dangerous now that she'd spent fifteen minutes stroking his ears. "Good night, Julian. I'm sorry you had to go to the bother of ruining both of our evenings!"

Dog and man followed her to the door. "I'll take you home, Emmy."

"That's not necessary," she protested quickly.

"I would be guilty of the worst possible manners if I were to send you out into the night alone." He pulled the leather jacket out of the closet and draped it around her shoulders. Then he reached for a heavy sweater for himself and politely opened the door.

Outside the fog swirled in thick white sheets. Emelina could barely see a foot in front of her face. Xerxes trotted outside as if it were broad daylight.

"I'll get a flashlight," Julian said, opening another cupboard. "Good thing you're only a block away, isn't it? Of course, you're welcome to spend the night, if you'd rather not venture out into this soup."

"No, no, I'll be fine."

"I was afraid you'd say that." His mouth lifted in wry humor. "Let's go."

Once outside it wasn't quite as bad as it had seemed. They made their way slowly along the street, which lacked anything as sophisticated as a sidewalk, until they arrived at the rundown picket fence that surrounded Emelina's cottage. At the door, Emelina turned and made a bid to dismiss her unwanted escort.

"Thank you very much, Julian. As you can see there was absolutely no need to trouble yourself this evening. Now that you've had the answers to your questions, I hope you'll leave me alone so that we can both go our separate ways."

He eyed her as if she were displaying a distressing amount of stupidity. "But you've hardly begun to answer my questions, Emmy," he corrected softly. "Surely you must see that. We have a great deal more to discuss, you and I. But it is getting late and I agree it's time you were home. Tomorrow, however, I think we will pick up this conversation where we left off."

"But I answered your questions!" she gasped furiously.

"Emmy, you only whetted my interest."

"But, Julian!"

He leaned forward and stopped her protest by brushing his mouth ever so lightly against her own. It was the gentlest of warnings, but Emelina got the message immediately. She shut up, stepped inside her door and slammed it closed behind her. She was trembling with reaction to the events of the evening and the hint of threat which had been left behind on her lips. Belatedly she realized she was still wearing Colter's jacket.

A little awkwardly she stepped away from the door, aware of the warmth of the leather and the way it carried a trace of Julian's scent. Quickly she shrugged out of it, alarmed by the strangely intimate sensation.

Outside in the thickening fog Julian made his way slowly back to the cottage he was renting. Xerxes paced faithfully at his heels, and Julian called to him softly.

"Good boy, Xerxes. Good boy." He paused and then murmured, "What did you think of her, pal?" The dog laughed silently up at him. "You liked her, didn't you? She's scared of you, though. She's scared of both of us. Probably heard all the talk in town. I wonder what she's really doing here on the coast. That story she told was pretty wild. On the other hand, I didn't get the feeling she was lying." Julian shook his head. "Interesting, isn't she? Intriguing."

He reached the cottage door and let himself and the dog inside, wondering if the woman had been telling him the truth. Had she really been out on the beach in the middle of the night doing undercover work to help her brother out of a blackmail jam? The astonishing part was that he could almost believe the ridiculous tale. There was something about the way she met his eyes, something about the way her rounded little chin lifted when she challenged him. She had the spirit and, he had a hunch, the imagination to get herself into trouble.

How many women of his acquaintance would undertake an exotic task such as she claimed to have set herself for the sake of helping a man, even a relative? Most of the ones he knew would have dissolved into hysterics at the notion of blackmail and probably not a single one would have found themselves on a deserted beach at midnight attempting a bit of breaking and entering.

Most of the people Julian Colter had encountered in his life didn't take loyalty to another human being to that extreme. The possibility that he might have come across a woman who saw nothing wrong in that sort of outmoded loyalty was more than intriguing.

It kept Julian awake for a good portion of what remained of the night.

Two

As a writer, Emelina told herself very early the next morning, she should take the attitude that every experience was grist for the mill. But as she tugged on a pair of jeans and reached for an emerald green velour sweater she found it difficult to view the experiences of the previous evening with the sort of objectivity required in order to use them in a story.

The memory of Julian Colter materializing out of the fog along with his Doberman still sent chills down her spine. It would be a while before she could write about that experience with a steady hand at the typewriter!

Still, she reminded herself resolutely as she tied the laces of her canvas shoes and reached for Colter's leather jacket, which was lying on the end of the couch, there was always the possibility of using that scene on the beach in some future novel. Yes, she would tuck it away in the back of her mind, and someday she might find it very useful.

Letting herself outside into the nippy morning air, Emelina draped the leather jacket across her arm and started down the narrow street to the cottage at the other end. She had awakened with the knowledge that she wanted Julian Colter's jacket out of her house as soon as possible.

Emelina couldn't explain her reaction to the intimacy implied by the jacket's presence in her cottage, but she couldn't ignore it, either. She wished she'd thought to return it to its owner the previous evening.

But Julian's brief, warning kiss had driven every thought from her mind except getting behind the safety of her own door. Emelina sighed and walked a little more quickly as she neared Julian's cottage. She could only hope Colter wasn't an early riser. Her plan was simple. She would leave the jacket hanging on the front doorknob and then leave without announcing her presence.

Unfortunately for the simplicity of her plan, Xerxes did prove to be an early riser. She heard his sharp, questioning bark as she slung the leather jacket over the knob. Before she could get off the front porch, the door opened.

Xerxes came bounding out, apparently enormously pleased to see her again. Julian stood in the doorway and watched his dog's greeting with calm amusement.

"Down, Xerxes," Emelina muttered, cautiously patting the dog's head as she stood with one foot on the bottom porch step. "That's a good boy. Down!" Having a Doberman trying to pounce on one was enough to make anyone a trifle anxious, she decided. Then she glanced up at Julian and decided that in this case the dog's owner was a source of greater anxiety.

"Good morning, Emmy. You're just in time for a cup of coffee."

"No!" she said instinctively, trying to edge down the path. "I mean, no thank you," she amended, remembering her manners. "I was just on my way into town for coffee. Thank you very much. I only stopped by to return your jacket."

Julian glanced down at the garment draped over the doorknob. "So I see. Well, since I now have a jacket, I think I'll come into town with you and buy you that cup of coffee. Come on, Xerxes. Back in the house. You'll get your morning walk a little later."

Xerxes looked wistfully at Emelina, who was astonished that a Doberman could assume such an expression, and then he loped obediently up the steps and back into the cottage. Julian closed the door on him and reached for his jacket.

"There's really no need to accompany me," Emelina began, racking her brain for a way out of the unexpected date. "I go into town every morning for coffee. It's quite safe and I'm used to it!"

"I know," Julian agreed gently, zipping up the jacket as he came down the steps. "I've seen you. I've been looking for an excuse to invite myself along, and this morning I have one, don't I?"

Emelina's eyes narrowed as she regarded him resentfully. "What excuse?" she challenged.

"Why, that we're more or less conspirators," he replied ingenuously, dark eyes laughing down at her as he fell into step beside her. "After finding you down on the beach last night trying to search that house I feel *involved.*"

She shot him a skeptical glance. "You're not involved and you know it. You're just bored and looking for a way to amuse yourself. You said as much last night!"

"Lucky for me you came along, hmmm? This morning I think I would like to hear the rest of the story, Emmy."

"What do you mean, the rest of the story? I told you what you wanted to know last night!" she protested. Angrily she glared straight ahead as they walked along the edge of the road into the quiet village. How was she going to get free of this dangerous man? Why on earth had he latched onto her like this?

"There are one or two details still missing," he explained easily.

"Such as?"

"Such as *why* your brother is being blackmailed."

Emelina's expressive mouth firmed. "That's none of your business."

He slanted her a cool glance. "Convince me," he ordered succinctly.

Her eyes widened in renewed nervousness. "I told you last night this has nothing to do with you," she whispered. Was he still thinking that somehow she was a threat to him? A Syndicate chief hiding out was bound to be more than normally suspicious, she realized unhappily.

"Like I said, convince me." Julian pushed open

the door of the coffee shop and ushered her into the pleasant, bustling warmth.

As he guided her toward a vacant booth Emelina felt the curious looks of the other patrons, most of them locals. A wave of new uneasiness assailed her as she slid reluctantly into the booth. There was no doubt but that the village folk would begin speculating at once on the fact that the single lady vacationer in town was having coffee with the mysterious Mob boss. Damn! Things were going from bad to worse in a hurry.

Julian seemed oblivious to the stares and muttered comments, but as she eyed him while he quietly ordered coffee, it occurred to Emelina that he undoubtedly knew very well what was being said around him. He was simply too arrogant to give a damn. Mafia types were undoubtedly *very* arrogant. Emelina winced at the thought and tried to tell herself that someday this would all make a really great manuscript.

"So let's hear it, Emmy. Why is your brother being blackmailed?"

She drew in her breath as the coffee arrived, poured a great deal of cream into her cup and decided the only chance of escape with a man like this was the truth. People like him would know at once if one were lying. She shivered.

"My brother is a very brilliant, very fast-rising executive with a large multinational conglomerate," she began in a tight voice. "He is in line for a vice-presidency and an important transfer to San Francisco."

Julian nodded, saying nothing as he sipped the steaming brew. His dark gaze never left her face.

"Eric Leighton appeared out of nowhere about a month ago. He had once been a...a close friend of my brother's."

"Some friend," Julian observed mildly, "to resort to blackmail."

"Yes." The single word of agreement was dragged from Emelina.

"But that's the thing about close friends and... others," Julian went on thoughtfully, "they often can't be trusted. Loyalty is a very rare commodity in this world."

"You ought to know," Emelina retorted without pausing to think.

He arched one brow.

"I mean, in your line of work and all. You've probably learned the hard way that you can't trust everyone," Emelina explained hurriedly, wishing she'd kept her mouth shut.

"About your brother," he prompted coolly.

"Yes, well, Leighton used to be very close to my brother and a handful of others. They were all friends in college, you see," she said carefully. "My brother was not always on the fast track to the executive suite, I'm afraid. At one time he was out to change the world. The quick way."

"Ah, I think I'm beginning to get a glimmering of understanding."

"Keith was very committed to his beliefs," she went on, edging her way closer to the core of the matter.

"In other words he was a flaming radical in college, out to change the world."

"Something like that," she admitted and then said loyally, "he believed in what he was doing at the time. He was very dedicated!"

"But he's since changed his mind?"

"Well, like everyone else, he's grown up and decided that the world can't be changed overnight. He's a very dynamic, hard-working person, and he has a lot of natural ability. The corporate world turned out to be a sphere in which he does very well. But he works for a very conservative, very staid company."

"And his bosses wouldn't look so kindly on him if they knew about his radical past?"

Emelina shook her head sadly. "And Eric Leighton, who hasn't done very well at all since he dropped out of college a few years ago, has decided he wants some of the success of his friends who have made it in the establishment. He's set up a very neat blackmailing scheme. For a price he'll keep his mouth shut about my brother's past."

"How did your brother react when Leighton approached him?"

Emelina lifted one shoulder. "Oh, he was all set to call in the cops and blow the whole thing wide open. But I convinced him that in the end he would suffer because Leighton was sure to make a point of exposing Keith's past to the world. I thought there might be another way to handle it. We know Leighton was involved with drugs in college. It was no secret at the time. My brother and I think he's probably still making a living by smuggling drugs or some related activity. We know he's never had a real job or tried to fit into society. Keith remembered that Leighton had once had a house on the Oregon coast. It was left to him by his parents. Leighton used to say it would make a good place to wait out the 'revolution.'"

"Which never came," Julian put in with a smile.

"Anyhow, Keith checked quietly with someone in the office of the local county recorder and found out that the house on the beach was still registered to Leighton. It occurred to me that it might be worth watching for a while. If he's involved in other illegal activities besides blackmailing old friends, there's a possibility he's using this secluded beach house for some aspect of his work."

"So you volunteered to come down here and spend a few weeks keeping the place under surveillance, is that it?" Julian asked, stirring his coffee absently.

"Something like that," Emelina confessed. She chewed her lip in a gesture characteristic of all her anxious moments. "Doesn't that sound like a logical sort of plan?" Nothing like getting advice from an expert, she told herself, watching him with a hopeful expression.

"Not particularly," Julian retorted, his mouth twisting wryly. "I think your brother had the right idea initially."

"Calling in the cops?" she exclaimed, shocked. "You think that was a good idea?" She couldn't imagine someone in Julian's line of work thinking it was ever a good idea to call in the police!

"They have their uses," he told her dryly, eyes narrowing.

"Well, it's out of the question. It would ruin my brother's career!"

"Blackmailers never go away, Emmy. You must have heard that by now. They'll go on bleeding a victim for as long as they can get away with it. You have to call the bluff."

"It's not a bluff," she whispered fiercely. "My brother's past, if it were known, would put his career in jeopardy. You don't understand how conservative his firm is! Oh, he probably wouldn't be fired or anything, but his superiors would almost surely lose interest in paving his way to the top. They would decide that basically he wasn't really their kind! Most of them came out of prestigious schools and were very careful to steer clear of campus political movements. They wouldn't *understand!*"

"You sound very concerned about your brother's welfare," Julian observed mildly.

"I am! He's my brother!"

"Your older brother or your younger brother?"

"My younger brother. He's twenty-nine, two years younger than me."

"Which is why he apparently let you talk him into this wild scheme to trap Leighton. He may be a fast-rising corporate man, but he's still a younger brother, with a younger brother's mentality, I suppose."

"What's that supposed to mean?" she demanded furiously.

"Only that he's accustomed to being bossed around by his older sister," Julian chuckled.

"You know nothing about my family or my relationship to my brother!"

Julian shook his head. "I know that, crazy as your plan undoubtedly is, you seem to mean well by it. You're determined to protect Keith, aren't you?"

"Well, of course, I am! He's my brother!" She stared at him, baffled that he should even make such an obvious statement.

Julian smiled. "Okay, I'll help you."

"You'll *what?*"

"Keep your voice down. Do you want everyone in town to know what you're doing?" he cautioned briefly.

Emelina tried to recover from her shock and force her mind to think in a rational fashion. Julian Colter's help was the very last thing she wanted. Help from a mysterious Syndicate boss would carry a very high price tag, indeed! "Thanks, but no thanks, Mr. Colter," she told him heatedly. "I prefer to handle this on my own."

"This kind of surveillance works better with two people."

She blinked. "It does?"

"Oh, definitely. Besides, my cottage is much closer to Leighton's house than yours is. It will be easier and less obvious if I handle part of the job of watching it."

For the life of her she couldn't read his expression. Emelina sat very still, running his logic through her head. He had a point, she told herself in consternation. And there was no doubt Julian Colter probably knew a great deal more about this sort of thing than she did. Then she shook her head, clearing away the deceptive reasoning. She must remember exactly who this man was and how very dangerous he could be. "Thank you, Julian," she said very formally, "but I don't want your help."

"Not even for your brother's sake?" he murmured.

She flinched. "It's just that I don't think it will be necessary to have outside assistance on this project. I'm perfectly capable of handling it by myself."

"Forgive me for saying this, Emmy," he drawled, "but I have the impression that while your plan has the merit of having been born of a vivid imagination, it might be lacking in one or two practical aspects. You don't really have any experience in this sort of thing, do you?"

"Well, no, but I don't see why it should be so difficult!"

"Look at the mess you got into last night. What if I had been Leighton?"

That shook her a little. "You weren't, so I don't see that it matters!" she managed staunchly.

He gave her a wry glance. "You're afraid to let me help, aren't you?"

"Frankly, yes."

"Why?"

Emelina clenched her teeth, striving for a polite response to the outrageous question. He must be very well aware of why she didn't want his help! "This is a personal matter and I don't want to involve strangers," she finally mumbled, not quite meeting his eyes.

"You've already involved me by telling me the whole story," he pointed out.

"For which I could kick myself," she groaned morosely.

He gave her a level look. "I didn't exactly give you much choice."

"No, you certainly didn't," she agreed. "Are you always this overbearing and intimidating?"

"Goes with the territory," he explained dryly.

Emelina shut her eyes briefly in dismay. "Yes, I suppose it does."

"Well?" he pushed with a hint of challenge.

"Well, what?" She glared at him. "Am I going to accept your too-generous offer? Not on your life!"

"Not even for the sake of your brother?" he murmured insinuatingly. "Doesn't your loyalty to him extend as far as engaging the best available expert?"

Emelina surged to her feet, aware that she was being pressured, and furious at the man in the booth for applying the pressure. Her eyes went almost green as she leaned over the table, palms planted firmly on the Formica. "I will say this one more time, Julian Colter," she hissed through her teeth. "I do not want your help. I don't need your help. This is my business and I will attend to it. I have no intention of finding myself under any obligation to someone like you. Have I made myself perfectly clear?"

Julian watched her over the rim of his coffee cup. His face was set and hard, and his dark eyes were pools of unfathomable danger. "Very clear."

"Good, I'm glad we understand each other!" Emelina straightened and turned on her heel, anxious to leave him far behind. But Julian's voice caught her just as she was about to stride toward the door.

"Keep in mind, Emmy, that whatever your fears

about me, I'm the one man in the neighborhood who might be able to really help your brother."

Emelina shoved open the cafe door, violently aware of the eyes of the local people following her out into the street. They couldn't have overheard Julian's last remark, of course, but they were bound to be deeply curious about her relationship to the mystery man in their presence.

Damn! Damn! Damn! What a disastrous turn of events! Head down, hands shoved into the pockets of her jeans, Emelina berated herself during the entire walk back to her cottage.

No one but a fool would deliberately get herself in debt to a man like Julian Colter! In debt to the Syndicate? The Mob? The Mafia? Whatever the proper term was, she sure as hell didn't need that kind of trouble!

Visions of movies and books she had read on the subject leaped into her mind. Newspaper stories of famous personalities who had found themselves obligated to an underworld figure haunted her as she let herself back into the cottage. Her vivid imagination found no end to the frightening images it could conjure from such material.

And then she thought of her brother. Keith had agreed to let her watch the Leighton house for a few weeks, but if at the end of that time nothing happened that could be useful in a fight against Eric Leighton, he was determined to turn the whole thing over to the authorities and let the chips fall where they might.

Emelina muttered another string of rather explicit oaths as she considered the damage that could be done to her brother's flourishing career if his past was brought up and used to embarrass him publicly. Her brother might be disgusted enough with Leighton to take his chances, but Emelina couldn't bear the thought of seeing everything he had worked for during the past few years go down the drain.

Keith deserved his success, and she was going to see that it wasn't ruined by a vicious, scheming blackmailer like Eric Leighton! Emelina began to pace the floor as she considered her options. Brow furrowed, she beat a steady path between the front window of the old cottage and the kitchen counter. She *had* to get something on Leighton. And she only had a few weeks in which to do it. Keith would take matters into his own hands if she didn't accomplish something quickly. It had been all she could do to convince him to let her try her own plan.

But there had been absolutely nothing to see during the past week. She had kept an earnest vigil, but unfortunately Julian Colter was right. It was impossible for one person to keep a round-the-clock surveillance project going.

Julian Colter. Why did the one person who offered help have to be *him?*

She was on the point of cursing her bad luck when Emelina happened to remember the expressions on the faces of the other diners in the coffee shop that morning. She had known exactly what was passing through their minds and she had a hunch Julian knew, as well. What was it like going through life drawing that kind of attention?

Well, it was his own fault. He shouldn't have chosen his particular line of work if he didn't care to cause such comment! Then again, perhaps he hadn't chosen it. Maybe it was something you were born into. Perhaps Julian had never had any real choice in the matter.

Her mind drifted off along that tangent for a while longer as she tried to picture a young Julian growing up as the heir apparent in a crime family. Distractedly she shook herself free of her musings and returned to the problem at hand. Julian Colter's life work was definitely not her concern.

Yet every time she reached the turnaround point on the floor in front of the bay window overlooking the ocean, Emelina found her mind returning to the subject of Julian Colter. He could help her. If anyone could, it would be he. Instinctively she was more certain of that than she had been of just about anything else in her life.

In debt to a man like that? What was she thinking of? Emelina Stratton knew what it meant to be in debt, but she'd never been involved in that sort of obligation!

Out of sheer desperation she grabbed her note pad and threw herself down on the lumpy couch in an effort to take her mind off her problem by focusing on her writing. After all, she had promised herself that in between trips to check on Leighton's house, she would do some real work here on the coast.

It was a pointless exercise. Her active imagination simply would not concentrate on the characters of her space gothic. It insisted on returning to the subject of the man in the cottage at the end of her street. And to the problem of helping her brother.

Julian Colter would probably know how to go about solving her brother's problem.

That one inescapable fact kept returning to tease and tug and cajole. Yes, he would know what to do, but what price would she wind up paying? She would have to make it absolutely clear that if she did accept his help, *she* was the one under an obligation to pay the tab, not her brother. Could one make deals like that with people like Colter? Would he honor his side of the bargain and hold only her responsible?

She could always ask him, couldn't she?

Emelina threw down her pen in a gesture of self-disgust. What was the matter with her? How could she even think of running such risks?

For her brother's sake, of course. Keith was closer to her than anyone else in the world. She rarely saw her beautiful but flighty mother, who had remarried and was happily living in luxury on the East Coast. Her father had disappeared during her junior year in college, leaving behind all those debts. Her marriage had been a disaster. Through it all Keith had been her friend as well as her brother.

What it all boiled down to was the simple fact that she would do anything she had to do in order to help him. And when she looked at the matter in its simplest terms, Emelina decided shortly after sunset that evening, the options narrowed considerably.

She needed the best available help, and she knew where to get it. There was no reason to hesitate any longer. Squaring her shoulders, Emelina dragged a striped Hudson Bay blanket-coat out of the closet and belted it on. Resolutely she turned up the high collar and pulled open the door of the cottage. She really had no choice.

The walk up the street was one of the longest Emelina had ever undertaken. It lasted forever and yet all too soon she was walking up the path to the slightly tilted porch of Julian's cottage.

Xerxes was aware of her before she could knock even once. She heard his expectant little whine and braced herself for his cheerful assault when the door opened.

"Ah, Emmy," Julian said, a wealth of satisfaction in his voice as he stood on the threshold and took in the sight of her standing on his front step. "I had a feeling you wouldn't disappoint me."

Emelina was too busy fending off Xerxes to get a good look at Julian's face but she thought she caught a trace of satisfaction in his eyes as well as his voice and didn't quite know what to make of it.

"Down, Xerxes," she ordered gruffly as the sleek dog danced around her. He shoved his head under her hand, and she was more or less obligated to pat him. The long pink tongue came out to thank her. "I've come to talk to you about...about my problem," she said to Julian as she hastily wiped her hand on her jacket.

"I assumed as much. Come in, Emmy. Have you eaten?"

"No, but I'm not really hungry," she assured him quickly.

"If you are going to accept my help, you might as

well accept my food,'' he pointed out with unassailable logic. ''And perhaps a drink, too, I think,'' he added as he shut the door behind her.

Emelina had a moment of panic as the door closed and she found herself trapped in the room with him. She made a frantic grab for her fortitude and nodded once. ''Yes, I think I could use the drink.''

Xerxes draped himself contentedly by the fire after seeing Emelina into the old stuffed chair she had used the previous evening. Silence reigned in the room until Emelina found a glass of deep red Zinfandel pressed into her hand. She took a long sip and then met Julian's eyes as he sat down across from her.

''There's just one thing,'' she stated very carefully. He gave her a politely inquiring look. ''My brother is not a part of this deal. I'm the one making the arrangement with you.''

''I understand,'' Julian said very gently.

Emelina would have given a lot of money in that moment to have had the gift of reading minds. What the devil was he thinking? ''I am the only one who will be required to repay your offer of help,'' she clarified, feeling as if she were digging her own grave.

He inclined his head in acknowledgment.

''Can I trust you?'' she whispered.

''You can trust me.'' It was a quiet statement of fact, and Emelina found herself believing him. There was no real reason to do so, yet she did. Perhaps men like this really did have their own code of honor. He saw her watching him and lifted his glass in salute. ''To our bargain, Emmy Stratton.''

They sipped the solemn toast in silence. For a long

moment there was only the crackle of the fire on the hearth and the pounding of Emelina's pulse as she absorbed the impact of what she had done. She couldn't seem to take her eyes off Julian's face. He was the personification of the devil, she told herself. Or perhaps it was Dracula he personified. Legend had it that such creatures could be strangely attractive to a woman.

Emelina's breath stopped for a split second as she realized just what she had been thinking. *Oh, no,* she screamed silently, *surely I'm not going to find myself in that kind of quicksand!* Her eyes widened. Attracted to Julian Colter? Never!

"What are you thinking, Emmy?"

"That when you sup with the devil you need a very long spoon," she replied with utter honesty. The old advice had never seemed so apropos. Getting close to Julian Colter was an excellent way to get one's fingers burned. Badly.

A strange little smile played at the edge of his hard mouth as he regarded her. "Since I want you to share my supper with me, I shall go and see just how long a spoon I can find," he murmured, rising lithely from the depths of the old chair.

Emelina was left to stare into the flames and wish she could have bitten out her tongue before speaking.

When Julian returned to the living room it was with a platter of sandwiches, two bowls of heated soup and a small salad. The speed with which it arrived made Emelina realize that it must have been ready before she had knocked on his door.

"You were expecting me?" she inquired rather

dryly, helping herself to a cheese and lettuce sandwich, even though she hadn't planned on accepting his food.

"Let's just say I was hoping you'd show up this evening."

They ate slowly, saying little. Emelina found the flames on the hearth unusually fascinating, and Julian seemed to think the same of her tightly drawn profile. Neither of them was inclined to go back to the business at hand.

"You're scared to death of me, aren't you, Emmy?" Julian said at last as they finished off the sandwiches.

"Hardly," she found the gumption to retort. She flicked a crust of bread in Xerxes's direction. "I'm just naturally cautious!"

He laughed at that, surprising her. It was the first time she'd heard him give way to humor to such an extent. It was at her expense, of course, she reminded herself crossly. Xerxes downed the bread crust and licked his chops politely.

"I don't think you're cautious at all, Emelina Stratton. Not when you're out to protect your brother. Would you offer that same loyalty to a lover, I wonder?"

"What?" Her head came up quickly as she stared at him in astonishment. The expression on his face held her absolutely still. She saw the deep, masculine curiosity and the restrained flicker of desire that had invaded the compelling dark eyes, and every instinct she possessed came abruptly to life. The result was a chaos of emotion and crossed signals that left her easy prey.

Julian Colter reached across the short space that divided them and tugged her effortlessly into his lap.

Three

"You've already found the courage to dine with the devil," Julian whispered deeply, his mouth hovering above hers. "Let's see if you have the courage to let him kiss you."

Emelina lay cradled across his thighs, one of his arms locked warmly around her. She was fiercely aware of a hypnotizing wonder. The attraction she had briefly recognized earlier in the evening was very real. *My God,* she thought bleakly, *why does it have to be with this man?*

Before she could summon the protest she knew she ought to make, Julian's hand lifted to frame the side of her face and hold her still for his kiss. She was aware of the heat of his fingers alongside her cheek and then came the far more intimate heat of his mouth.

How could a kiss be at once marauding and persuasive? Demanding, yet coaxing? How could a man like this kiss a woman as if she were an infinitely valuable and precious creature? Where Emelina expected rough aggression she received sensual insistence. Where she expected dominance she received warm inducement.

The dichotomy was spellbinding. Emelina closed her eyes, not daring to move as his lips teased hers. She felt his fingers slide upward into her braided hair, pressing her head close to his shoulder. Then came the tip of his tongue outlining her trembling mouth. Gently, insistently, persuasively, that tongue moved, his lips nibbling at hers until, with a soft little moan, Emelina succumbed to the sensual demand and allowed him into her warmth.

She felt rather than heard the growl deep in his throat as he hungrily invaded the territory she had ceded. The fingers in her hair began to thread and twist until she was vaguely aware that her braid had been undone. Beneath the searching impact of his kiss she stirred at last, instinctively seeking safety when it was far too late.

As if sensing her belated wariness, Julian deepened the embrace, filling her mouth with the provocative taste of his own. When her hand fluttered anxiously to his shoulder he released his grip on her hair to catch her fingers and guide them up to the coal darkness of his own heavy pelt. When he released them her hands were somehow entwined in the depths of his hair.

"Emmy, sweet Emmy. Don't be afraid of me. Give me what I want. You're so intriguing, so soft..." The words came lingeringly, persuasively as he reluctantly broke the contact of their mouths to seek the line of her throat.

"Julian, Julian, *please.*" But in that moment Emelina couldn't have said what it was she wanted from him. Her eyelids were squeezed tightly shut as if to block out the strange reality of what was happening and her ambergold nails scored the nape of his strong neck.

"I've been watching you for days," he breathed huskily, his palm sliding down her throat to her shoulder. "Wondering about you, speculating, playing guessing games with myself. The closer I get, the more you intrigue me."

"It's only that you're bored out here in the middle of nowhere," she began, but he interrupted her with rough certainty.

"Hush, Emmy, you don't know what you're talking about." And then his hand trailed boldly downward to the curve of her full breast and closed over it with a possessiveness that should have annoyed her violently.

Emelina couldn't find the scathing protest she needed. Instead she gasped softly and turned her face into his shoulder, pressing close to the comfort of the wool plaid shirt he wore. Her fingers at the nape of his neck clenched almost convulsively and she heard his sigh of masculine pleasure.

"A man could lose himself in your softness, Emmy," he growled as if he half resented, half longed for exactly that fate. Gently he explored the shape of her, and she sensed his growing impatience at the resistance offered by the bra she wore beneath her velour top.

Slowly his hand released her and drifted farther downward until he found the hem of the emerald sweater. Emelina flinched as he slid his fingers inside and discovered the warmth of her skin.

When he felt her start of uncertainty Julian tightened his hold, urging her closer. She was suddenly aware of the hardness of his thighs beneath her, felt the gathering male tension in his body. Once again Emelina told herself she must break free of the seductive web he was weaving, but just as she found the strength to try pulling back, he found the clasp of her bra and released it.

In the next moment the weight of her breast was filling his hand, and Emelina moaned again, this time with the desire that was springing to life in her loins. What was it that attracted her to a man like this? How on earth could a dangerous devil like Julian Colter overwhelm the defenses that had stood for years?

When his thumb grazed over a nipple, coaxing it forth, a melting warmth began to flow through her veins. She knew herself capable of a reasonable level of affection, but she had never thought of herself as a particularly sensual woman. There had never been a man who could quicken her senses this way. The casual approach her husband had taken to sex had left her disappointed and unenthusiastic about the intimate embrace. Since the end of her marriage, it had been an easy matter to keep her physical relationships with men on a safe level. She had not even been tempted to allow a man into her bed.

But, then, she hadn't known real temptation, Emelina realized suddenly. This was the genuine article. This pulsating, beckoning, melting sensation Julian was creating in her. *This* was real temptation. The danger in Julian Colter lay not only in his profession, but in the incredible effect he had on her.

"No," Emelina finally managed in a rasping, throaty voice as she tried to resist what was happening. "Julian, please stop."

"But I want you so, sweet Emmy. I need you tonight. Can't you feel the need in me? Be generous with me." He circled the now-firm bud of her nipple with the tip of one finger while his lips moved along her throat. His voice poured over her senses like warm honey.

"Julian, I can't," she whispered achingly.

"You feel so good under my hands. How can I let you go?" The hand on her breast shifted at last and flattened boldly against the soft curve of her stomach. He raised his head and sealed her mouth once more with his own as if to forestall the protest she would make when he began fumbling with the fastening of her jeans.

Emelina did attempt a protest. She stiffened immediately as the intimacy of the gentle assault made itself known. She must not let him go any further. She mustn't. But the cry was locked forever in her throat as his tongue filled her mouth. Then his fingers were undoing the zipper of her jeans and stroking the nylon of her panties.

Panic finally rose within her, overriding the sensual glow created by his touch. Emelina planted her hands on his chest and shoved, breaking the contact between them at last. The effort left her breathless, her heart pounding.

"No, Julian. Stop it. I don't want any more of this."

He stilled, his dark eyes assessing her wary hazel gaze and the trembling curve of her softened mouth. "Is this the limit of your courage, then?" he teased gently.

"Definitely," she retorted as stoutly as possible. He didn't seem angry, she thought in silent relief. Perhaps he would be manageable after all. Was the devil ever really manageable, though? Or did he simply choose to appear that way on occasion when it suited him?

"I think you underestimate yourself, Emmy," Julian murmured, bending his head to brush his lips lightly across her forehead.

"Let me go, Julian."

"Is that really what you want me to do?"

"Yes," she whispered. "I want to go home."

"And I want to keep you here all night."

"You can't!"

He hesitated a long moment and Emelina wondered desperately what he was thinking. She sensed his own inner conflict and wondered at it. It was difficult to imagine a man like this being torn by conflicting emotions. There was a wistfulness in his expression that abruptly reminded her of Xerxes. Sleek, lethal creatures such as these two had no business looking wistful!

"All right, Emmy, I'll take you home."

She hid her astonishment at the surprisingly easy victory, wriggling quickly off his lap as he released her. Hastily, turning her back to him, she adjusted her clothing and tried to tame the wild mane of her chestnut hair which tumbled now in disarray.

"Emmy?" She didn't turn around. "Emmy, there's no one else, is there?"

It was more a statement of fact than a question. Emelina tightened her lips, wondering if she could pull off a quick lie. It would be best if he thought that there was someone else. There might be some measure of safety in having him believe that. "Believe it or not, I do have a rather active social life," she began flippantly, fastening her jeans.

He was on his feet and suddenly very close behind her. His arms came around her waist and his face buried itself in her hair. "Emmy? Please don't tease me or lie to me. Just tell me the truth."

Her mouth went quite dry with a nameless fear. Why should she worry about telling the truth to a man like this? On the other hand, she wasn't a very good liar. His arms tightened, pulling her back against his still-aroused body. Emelina took the warning at face value.

"No," she got out huskily. "There's no one else. Not anymore."

"There was once?" he persisted gently.

"I'm divorced," she declared starkly.

"So am I."

"Oh." She wasn't quite sure what to say next.

"Which leaves us both free, doesn't it?"

Emelina was silent, mentally searching for a way out of the trap.

"Doesn't it, Emmy?"

"What are you trying to do?" she demanded bitterly. "Make me acknowledge that somehow because I don't currently have a lover, I'm fair game?"

He spun her around at that and suddenly, for the first time, Emelina saw anger in his night-dark gaze. It froze her to the spot, sending a chill down her spine.

"I was simply making an observation," Julian ground out slowly. "The fact that both of us are free is going to make things easier, but if you did happen to have a current lover, it wouldn't have made any real difference. I'd still want you and I would still do my best to make you want me. Do you understand?"

"Yes, I most certainly do," she flung back recklessly. "You're saying you'd still consider me fair game whether or not I had commitments elsewhere! Of all the arrogant, unethical, contemptible..."

The anger went out of his eyes to be replaced by rueful amusement as Julian firmly silenced her with a palm across her mouth. Above the edge of his hand her eyes continued to berate him, but he only shook his head. "Please, Emmy, that's enough for tonight. You'll hurt my feelings!"

"Hah!" she muttered scornfully as he removed his hand. "I doubt that you have many feelings other than...than the kind you just exhibited while you were kissing me," she concluded a little lamely.

"You mean other than sexual feelings?" he suggested helpfully. "Well, I will admit to those." He glanced down at the still-taut outline of his own body, and Emelina was horrified to find her glance automatically following his. Hurriedly she wrenched her eyes away from the sight of his hardened frame and turned to stare fixedly into the flames of the fire. "But I do have other kinds of feelings, too, Emmy," he added softly.

"I think I'd like to go home now," she stated remotely.

"Very well." Without further protest he collected his jacket and hers and whistled to Xerxes. "Let's go."

Julian saw her politely to her door and waited until he'd heard her lock it before he reluctantly started back to his own cottage with Xerxes at his heels. He was wryly aware of the steady ache in his lower body. Emelina would never know how close he had come to overriding all her nervous objections tonight. He'd wanted her. Very badly. Julian set his teeth as the night breeze off the ocean caught his hair and chilled him.

Perhaps the chill would calm his tight body, he decided moodily. With luck it would have the same effect as a cold shower. Damn it, but it had been a long time since he'd wanted a woman this suddenly, this positively. His hands curved unconsciously as he remembered the soft roundness of her breast and thigh.

He knew what it meant to desire a woman physically, but he was rapidly coming to realize that what he wanted from Emelina Stratton amounted to something much more complicated than physical satisfaction. Face it, he told himself grimly, he wanted a large chunk of that loyalty she was prepared to give someone she loved. He wanted to know what it was like to have a woman who was loyal to him completely. A woman who would stand with him against the world if need be. A woman who would give herself completely to him.

Now he had struck a bargain with a woman who seemed quite prepared to honor her end of it. What would she do when he called in the tab? Would she really pay the price he was beginning to think he would demand? Would she repay him with the loyalty and honor and faithfulness he craved?

God! He was turning fanciful as he neared forty, Julian decided in mocking self-disgust. Had he come to this isolated place only to suffer through a mid-life crisis? What was the matter with him? Emelina Stratton owed him nothing at all. At least, not yet.

And even if he could manage to ensure that she was in his debt, how could he also ensure that she would repay him in the way he wanted?

Well, first things first. Step number one was to seal the bargain as thoroughly as possible. She had only allowed herself to risk getting this close to him because she thought he might be able to help her get her brother out of the blackmailing mess. He'd better see what he could do about that little detail!

When Xerxes automatically trotted toward the path leading up to the cottage, Julian whistled him back onto the road and together they walked to the edge of the bluff to stare down at the empty beach house which belonged to Eric Leighton.

For a long moment Julian stood there, the leather

collar of his jacket turned up around his neck, his hands buried in the fleece-lined pockets. Broodingly he considered the house and the story Emelina had told him. He no longer doubted her tale, but there was every reason to doubt her wild plan of keeping an eye on Leighton's beach house. His woman had one hell of a vivid imagination, Julian decided, his mouth twisting indulgently.

His woman. The words rang through his head as he realized how right they sounded.

"I'd better give her the feeling I'm working on this ridiculous project," he muttered to Xerxes, who glanced up inquiringly. "Tomorrow night we'll take her back down to that beach house and have a look inside. There probably won't be any great clues lying around on the floor, but at least she'll think I'm making some effort to carry out my end of the deal."

And it was vital that she believe he could be trusted to honor his end of the bargain, Julian thought as he turned back toward his own cottage. He wanted her thoroughly committed to him.

The memory of his inner satisfaction earlier that evening when he'd opened his door to find her on his front step returned as Julian slid into bed sometime later. He lay back against the pillow, his arms behind his head, and stared up at the ceiling. He'd been right to try to lure her with an offer of help. Her loyalty to her brother was deep enough to make her strike the bargain.

There was a certain mental satisfaction in seeing the progress of his plans, but that didn't altogether compensate for the physical dissatisfaction of his body, Julian realized grimly. He went to sleep wanting Emelina in his bed.

Emelina did her best to throw off the aftereffects of Julian's lovemaking, but the next morning she felt curiously hungover. There was a new restlessness in her that had nothing to do with the task she had undertaken for her brother. *Why did it have to be Julian Colter who had done this to her?*

Gloomily she made a pot of coffee and sat in front of her window, drinking it. There was no point rehashing the events of the preceding evening. She'd spent half the night doing exactly that. What was the matter with her? She had made a bargain with the man, but she certainly didn't want to feel this compelling, uneasy attraction to him. Matters were dangerous enough as they stood!

She heard Xerxes before she heard the knock on her door. The cheerful yip of the Doberman made her grimace. That dog was as bad as his master. He seemed determined to make her like him. Emelina didn't care for Doberman pinschers anymore than she cared for mobsters!

"Oh, good morning, Julian," she managed weakly as she opened the door. His eyes went accusingly to the cup of coffee in her hand.

"Xerxes and I didn't see you go by on your way into town for your usual morning cup of coffee."

"Er, that's because I decided to have it here instead." She could hardly tell him she hadn't wanted to risk walking past his house and having him join her once more. Emelina thought of the staring eyes yesterday morning in the cafe and winced.

"Do you make good coffee?" Julian asked unabashedly.

Emelina could have groaned aloud. "No," she tried hopefully. It didn't daunt him.

"Well, I'm not too fussy." He waited expectantly.

"Will you have a cup?" she asked in resignation.

"Thought you'd never ask." He was striding inside, ordering Xerxes to lie down on the hearth rug, before she could blink an eye. "Actually, I came by to ask if you'd like to go with me tonight when I walk down to Leighton's house to have a look around," he went on conversationally as he settled into the overstuffed chair by the window.

"Oh, yes!" For the first time that morning Emelina knew a burst of genuine enthusiasm. "When are we going?" She quickly poured out his coffee.

"Around sunset, I think, so we won't have to use flashlights. They might draw attention if someone should happen to notice the light in a vacant house." He accepted the mug she handed to him and sipped cautiously. His eyes narrowed as he swallowed. "You were right," he told her dryly.

Her brow went up as she sank into the seat across from him. "About my coffee? I warned you." She took another taste of her powerful brew.

"I can see why you've been walking into town for a cup every morning!"

"If you don't like my coffee, you're free to leave," Emelina pointed out testily.

"I wouldn't think of being so rude," he retorted manfully. "But tomorrow morning you must allow me to take you back into town or make a pot myself!''

For some reason Emelina's sense of humor asserted itself. ''Love me, love my coffee,'' she taunted lightly, blue green eyes laughing at him.

''I thought the phrase was 'love me, love my dog,''' he tossed back easily, but there was a gleam in his eyes.

''Not a chance.'' She flicked a wary glance at the quiet Doberman. ''Dogs like that weren't made to be loved.'' Emelina's momentary humor faded as she continued to stare at Xerxes, who lifted his head to stare back. ''They're bred for savagery. Trained to be guard dogs, sometimes killers.''

''I don't think you fully understand Xerxes. Or me.''

Whatever Emelina might have said to that was forestalled by Xerxes, who, aware that attention was on him, got lithely to his feet and padded across the room to thrust his head into Emelina's lap. Intelligent brown eyes met hers pleadingly. There wasn't anything she could do except reluctantly pat the animal.

''If I learned to tolerate your coffee, could you learn to tolerate my dog?'' Julian inquired a little too softly, watching her intently.

''We've already struck one bargain between us, Julian. Let's leave it at that.'' Emelina downed the last of her own coffee and leaped to her feet to get some more.

He didn't stay long. Perhaps he was afraid of wearing out his welcome, Emelina thought dully as she watched Julian and the Doberman head back down the street. She ought to be happy to see the last of him for the day, but somehow when he left her cottage he managed to take the excitement and warmth out of the old place. It was an excitement and warmth he had brought with him, she realized with an uncomfortable sense of wonder.

When Julian returned it was almost sunset. He was wearing a pair of jeans and an old flannel shirt and he'd left Xerxes behind. "I don't think we'll be needing him," he told Emelina as she came down the step to meet him. "He'd only be in the way on a venture like this. Besides, he'd probably leave paw prints in the dust on the floor." He scanned her jeans and close-fitting sweater approvingly.

"What about us? Won't we leave tracks, too?" Emelina walked quickly beside him, frowning intently into the distance.

"We'll be careful. With any luck the place will be furnished with a lot of old throw rugs like our cottages are. They won't show footprints. I hope."

Emelina chewed on her lower lip. "Julian, do you think it's safe to be doing this?"

"Safer than it was for you to be doing it alone at midnight!" he growled feelingly. "You were an idiot to go down there alone that night, you know," he continued matter-of-factly. "Anyone could have spotted your flashlight and followed you!"

"Someone did," she pointed out wryly.

He shot her a quick glance. "Be grateful it was I," he told her repressively.

She had the distinct impression she had managed to annoy Julian. For some perverse reason that thought served to lift her spirits. Or perhaps it was only anticipation of the approaching adventure. "Have you burgled many houses, Julian?" she asked chattily as they started down the path to the beach.

"We're not going to burglarize the place. We're only going to search it," he muttered.

"There's a difference?"

"About ten years in prison!"

"Have you ever been to prison, Julian?"

"No, I have not! Good grief, woman. You have a rather low opinion of me, don't you?" he complained half under his breath.

"I was just curious."

"Well, that's something, I suppose. Better to have you curious than indifferent." Before she could think of a response to that line, he was drawing her around to the side of the house that faced the ocean. "Now, I don't think anyone up on the bluff can see us, even if there happens to be someone looking this way," he explained, surveying the window with a critical eye.

"Can you open the window without breaking it?"

"It doesn't look very well latched. Pretty old. It will probably give with the right amount of pressure."

"Like everything else in your world?" she asked quietly.

He turned slowly, his dark glance cool and intimidating. With elaborate casualness he folded his arms and leaned back against the side of the weathered house. Quite suddenly Emelina wondered if she might have transgressed too far with that last thoughtless crack. As she always did when she was nervous, she chewed on her lower lip, her hazel eyes going almost green.

"Unless you'd like some real pressure applied to your nicely rounded backside, Emelina Stratton, you'd better control your new-found urge to provoke me."

Emelina blinked. Was that what she was trying to do? Provoke him? Perhaps. It was a small method of retaliating for this damn bargain he'd foisted on her. Or had she suddenly discovered an inexplicable desire to taunt him for other reasons?

"I'll behave, Julian," she drawled with syrupy politeness. "I didn't realize you were so easily offended."

He straightened away from the side of the house and turned back to the project of prying open the old window frame. "I'm not easily offended. It's just that I have the distinct feeling I'd better draw some lines or you'll be running roughshod over me!"

"Coward," she couldn't resist mumbling.

The window opened eventually under protest. Emelina felt her sense of excitement build rapidly as Julian went in first and then helped her over the ledge. As she stood gazing around at the shadowy interior of Eric Leighton's beach cottage, Emelina's first reaction was one of dismay.

"It looks like your cottage or mine!" she complained. Indeed, it contained the same sort of tattered and worn furniture, the same faded rugs and had the same weathered look as all the other beach houses.

"Well, what did you expect? A pile of cocaine sitting on the hearth waiting to be shipped out?" Julian asked calmly, stepping from rug to rug as he made his way toward the kitchen.

"Something like that, at least!" she retorted, glaring at his back.

His mouth crooked wryly. "Stay on the rugs and let's have a look around. I'll take the kitchen. You can start on the bedrooms."

There was only one bedroom and it contained nothing but a slanting bed and a chipped dresser. Emelina searched carefully and diligently, and when she was finished Julian went through the room, himself. They did each of the small rooms in the same fashion, but it soon became obvious that nothing in the nature of startling evidence was going to come to light.

"What about loose floorboards or secret safes in the walls?" Emelina demanded forty-five minutes later as she carefully tugged open a hall cupboard.

"What about them?" Julian growled, turning to see what she might find in the cupboard. "Do you want me to pry up every floorboard?"

"I suppose not," she sighed, frowning at the collection of neatly folded brown paper bags stacked on the bottom shelf of the cupboard. "Looks like Leighton is the compulsively thrifty type who saves all his paper bags."

"Yeah?" Curious, Julian came to stand behind her as they stood staring into the cupboard. "I wonder why?" He reached down to flip through them.

"Some people are that way." She shrugged. "You know the kind. They save every plastic bag from the produce department and fold every paper bag they take home from the store. Also, Leighton was into saving trees for a while, as I recall. He and Keith were rabid on the subject of environmentalism for a time.''

''Did you ever actually meet Leighton?''

''Once or twice.'' Emelina lifted one shoulder. ''There's nothing all that memorable about him. He lacked the charisma it takes to make it as a truly successful radical leader, and he tried to make up for it in other ways.''

''Like dealing dope?'' Julian murmured.

''It made him a big man on campus for a while. Gave him a feeling of importance. Keith began drawing away from him after he realized the direction Leighton was going.''

''Your brother wasn't part of the drug scene?'' Julian drawled.

''Absolutely not!'' Emelina defended her brother hotly. ''He was into health foods and meditation, not drugs!''

Julian looked at her wonderingly. ''This brother of yours, I take it, has never done anything wrong?''

''Nothing *really* wrong,'' she emphasized firmly.

''Uh huh. But he's still nervous about what Leighton could use to blackmail him? There must have been something, Emmy.''

''I told you, his present employer just wouldn't understand about the protest rallies and the radical politics and some of the other stuff. He never did anything wrong, Julian, he just lived a very unconventional lifestyle. That's all! But it would be enough to embarrass him now.'' There were the six months Keith had spent in that crazy commune, for example, she thought fleetingly. She could just imagine how that would go down with Keith's sixty-year-old mentor in the corporate offices!

"I get the feeling you'd stick by Keith even if it turned out he had gotten into something he shouldn't have," Julian said.

"Anyone can make a mistake, Julian," she admonished. "Which is not to say my brother made any really serious ones," she added quickly.

"I give up," he said with a half-smile. "It's clear you'd defend him regardless of what he did or didn't do." Julian shut the cupboard door on the stack of folded paper bags. "Come on, it's getting dark. We'd better get out of here."

"But we haven't found anything."

"It was an off-chance that we would, honey," he soothed. "Surely you realized that? Even if Leighton were using this place for illegal purposes he wouldn't be likely to leave evidence behind."

"I was so hoping to find something, though. I guess all we can do now is keep an eye on the place for the next few weeks and see if anything suspicious happens."

"Yes," he agreed, not looking at her. "I suppose that's one thing we should do."

"What else?" she asked eagerly as they climbed back out the window and Julian checked to make sure no obvious hand prints remained on the frame.

"Well, I could make a few inquiries."

"I see." Visions of Julian putting the far-reaching tentacles of his Mafia contacts into operation made her shudder involuntarily. It was frightening dealing with this kind of power. She must keep reminding herself just what she had gotten into by making the bargain with him. Sometimes, such as during the past hour, she almost forgot. He seemed so very *human.*

Julian saw the distant speculation in her eyes as they started toward the path to the bluff. He could just imagine the images her active imagination was conjuring up now. But there was one point he wanted to make before he saw her back inside her own cottage and returned to his lonely bed. His mouth hardened as he tried to find the words.

"You realize," he stated coolly, "that we're partners in crime now?"

She frowned. "What are you talking about?"

"We just illegally entered and searched that house. It's private property, Emelina. We had no right to be in Leighton's beach place."

"So?" She moved uneasily ahead of him to climb the path.

"So, I just want you to realize how involved you're getting in something that is not exactly legal."

"Are you trying to tell me we're following the same trail as Bonny and Clyde?" she tried to say flippantly.

"In hope we'll come to a better end than they did," he retorted dryly.

Belatedly Emelina remembered that in the legend of Bonny and Clyde the two outlaws hadn't lived long. They had died as violently as they had lived. "I shall rely on your professionalism to keep us out of serious danger, Julian," she told him bracingly.

"You're missing the point, Emmy," he said bluntly as he took her arm to start down the street.

"I'm trying to make you see that we're more or less committed to see this through together now. By breaking into that house with me, you helped seal our bargain a little more thoroughly. Do you understand?"

She pulled her arm out of his grasp, coming to a halt to stare up at him in surprise. "Did you think that I'd try to wriggle out of our deal?" she demanded proudly. "Is that the real reason you took me with you this evening? So I'd commit an illegal act with your assistance and feel committed to our bargain? You're a very devious man, Julian Colter, but for your information, you outfinessed yourself. I have no intention of backing out of our arrangement. I was *committed* to this project before you ever came along, remember?"

He watched her face in the disappearing light. "I want you to realize that you're committed to me, not just the project."

She drew away from him, her nerves on edge. "Don't you think I'm aware of that? I know what I've done by accepting your offer of help, Julian," she whispered tightly. "I always pay my debts. You don't have to worry. I'll make good on the tab when you present it."

Emelina turned and fled toward her cottage.

Four

It was Xerxes who caught Emelina as she tried to sneak into the village for coffee the next morning. She groaned softly to herself as the black-and-tan dog gave a joyful yip of greeting and bounded down from the front step where he'd been sitting. A quick glance assured Emelina that Julian was not in sight, so she spoke hurriedly to the enthusiastic animal.

"Down, boy! Go back. Back to the house. Do you hear me?" She tried to speak gruffly and to infuse her tone with command, but Xerxes seemed to miss the point. He whined and put his head in the neighborhood of her hand, looking up at her with that wistful glance that seemed so out of place on both him and his master.

"Back, Xerxes!" she tried again, but when he wriggled his ears suggestively she sighed and scratched them for him.

Julian's voice broke into the small scene, and Emelina whirled to see him topping the crest of the bluff. He'd been down on the beach near Leighton's house apparently. Xerxes must have beaten him back to the cottage. "It doesn't work if you give him mixed signals," he told her in mild amusement. "You have to be firm. Telling him to go back to the house while you're petting him at the same time only confuses him."

"He doesn't look confused," she noted dryly, glancing back down at the dog. Xerxes made an excellent excuse not to study Julian in the morning light. The wind-tossed dark hair with its iron gray strands, the lithe, strong figure cloaked in jeans and the familiar leather jacket, looked too appealing to her this morning. The last thing she wanted to do, Emelina reminded herself nervously, was find Julian Colter appealing.

"He's not confused, because he knows which signal is the more important one, I guess," Julian decided as he reached the pair. "Being petted is bound to outrank being ordered away from you."

"Silly dog," she muttered, "why don't you go find some stranger to attack?"

"Personally, I'm grateful to him," Julian drawled. "If he hadn't stopped you out here on the road, you would have gone right on into town without me, wouldn't you?"

"With any luck," Emelina agreed under her breath.

"Shame on you. And after giving me your word you'd allow me to buy you decent coffee this morning."

"Did I?" Emelina flushed guiltily, trying to remember the conversation. "I don't recall giving you my word on the subject," she said slowly.

"Well, it was definitely implied," Julian said briskly before quietly ordering Xerxes back to the house. "Come on, Xerxes. Inside. You're delaying my morning coffee."

Emelina frowned. Damn it, she hadn't implied anything of the kind as she recalled. But it was too late to argue. Julian was already falling into step beside her and there was really no alternative except to agree to his company. He would be even more difficult to send back to the house than Xerxes had been!

"What were you doing down at Leighton's house?" she inquired abruptly as they approached the cafe.

"Just thought I'd take another look around. Something's bothering me and I can't put my finger on it."

Emelina glanced up quickly. "What is it that's bothering you?"

"I'm not sure. The feeling I got about that cottage. Something doesn't fit." Julian smiled at her as he opened the cafe door. "Don't worry about it. I'm the one who's supposed to do the worrying, remember?"

The covert glances and the instant of speculative silence that greeted Emelina as she walked into the cozy coffee shop beside Julian raised the hair on the nape of her neck. Yesterday her response to the curiosity and questions around her had been a distinct uneasiness, tinged with embarrassment. This morning, for some reason, her reaction was one of haughty anger. Unconsciously she straightened her shoulders and lifted her chin in subtle challenge as she walked beside Julian to an empty booth.

Who the hell did these people think they were to be so rude? Julian wasn't bothering them. Whatever his profession may have been, here on the Oregon coast he was just another vacationer. Besides, she had made a pact with him. Like it or not, that seemed to put her in his corner, Emelina realized as she took her seat.

"Stop glaring at that fisherman at the counter," Julian advised gently as the waitress approached.

"He's staring at you."

"So?"

"So, it's rude! He has no business staring at you!" she hissed.

"He's curious," Julian explained off-handedly and then turned to give their order to an equally curious waitress.

Emelina sat back against the cushion and watched Julian's harshly carved profile as he dealt with the waitress. "Doesn't it bother you?" she finally asked hesitantly as the waitress disappeared. "The curiosity and the speculation, I mean?"

"Not particularly. I don't much care what these people think about me."

"You're so arrogant," she murmured, moving her head in a gesture of outright wonder. "You wouldn't bother to explain yourself to these people even if you were the president of a bank instead of a..." Her voice trailed off rather abruptly, and Emelina turned a rather fiery shade of red.

"Instead of what, Emmy?" he prompted, dark eyes amused.

"Never mind," she retorted aggressively. "How long are you going to stay here on the coast, Julian?" Anything to change the conversation!

"I haven't decided."

Which probably meant he didn't know how long it would take until it was safe to go back to his regular haunts, Emelina thought knowingly. "Where do you come from, Julian?"

"Arizona."

Emelina nodded morosely. She'd heard rumors about the underworld figures who had moved to the sunbelt.

"Any other questions?" Julian inquired politely as the coffee arrived.

Since she was unable to think of any "safe" questions, Emelina shook her head and gulped hot coffee. Her eyes followed the waitress vengefully.

"You can stop glaring at the waitress," Julian advised dryly.

"She's talking about you to that fishing person." Emelina kept on glaring at the woman until the waitress realized she was under unfriendly scrutiny and, flushing slightly in embarrassment, went to pour coffee at the end of the counter.

"Let her talk. What are you thinking of doing? Racing over there and beating both of them up because they're speculating about me?"

"It's not funny, Julian."

He shrugged, apparently unconvinced. "Can I ask

you a few questions now?" he went on with exaggerated civility.

"Like what?"

"Like why you're not married any longer," he said calmly, astonishing her.

"That's a very personal question!"

He shrugged again. And waited. There was a quality about his waiting that made Emelina shift uneasily in her seat. This man could be intimidating without half trying, she thought resentfully. "Julian, the only thing I got out of my marriage was a pile of debts that had to be paid off. It is not a subject I like to discuss, especially with strangers!"

"I'm hardly a stranger, am I?" The glance he gave her was a little like the kind she was beginning to expect from Xerxes. Why she bothered to respond to either creature was totally mystifying. "What sort of debts?" he pressed.

"My husband had taken out a lot of loans to cover his expenses in college and graduate school. He had expensive tastes," she added, remembering the Corvette and the handsome clothes. "When he left me, I had to drop out of college to pay off his bills." She grimaced and turned to stare out the window. "It seems like I've spent half my life paying off debts!"

"Who else saddled you with them?"

"My father was always overextended," she murmured, remembering her laughing, good-natured, horribly irresponsible parent. "It finally got to be too much, even for him, so he pulled a disappearing act a few years ago and left Keith and me to pick up the pieces. My mother is very much like him in temperament. Fortunately she's remarried into money!'' She swung her head back to find Julian studying her. ''I have excellent credit references, Julian,'' she told him with a trace of bitterness. ''You don't have to worry that I won't pay you.''

''Even though what I ask for won't have anything to do with cash?'' He continued to watch her with that steady, assessing glance.

''Could we talk about something else?'' she pleaded.

''If you like.''

''Why aren't you still married, Julian?'' she dared, feeling that he owed her some personal history in exchange for the background information he'd pried out of her.

''My wife ran off with another man,'' he explained very simply.

''I see.'' She wished she'd resisted the urge to ask.

''The other man was once my best friend and business partner,'' he continued roughly.

''Oh, Julian!'' Eyes widening with dismay, Emelina stared at him. ''How awful for you! No wonder you're so concerned about...about...''

''About loyalty and commitment?'' he filled in for her. ''Yes.''

''What happened to them?''

''My ex-wife and my ex-friend? Why do you ask?''

Emelina glanced away. ''I just wondered. It occurred to me that you might have felt, er, vengeful.''

''I did. For a while.''

She wondered if he'd taken steps to carry out some

terrible Mafia-style revenge. Her mind fashioned an almost unlimited series of possibilities based on several violent books she had read. She decided not to ask any further questions on the subject. "I was going to pick up some groceries and my mail," she went on deliberately, seeking a way to draw the intimate discussion to an end.

Julian nodded, setting down his cup. "Good idea. I'm having my mail forwarded here, too. But I have an alternative suggestion as far as the groceries are concerned."

"What's that?"

"Let's choose them together. We can have dinner at my place tonight."

Emelina knew a command when she heard one, and somehow she couldn't seem to summon the strength of purpose to ignore it. "All right."

"Is your coffee a sample of your culinary talents?" he teased as they rose from the table.

"If you're worried about being stuck with all the cooking, you needn't be," she retorted hotly. "I make a really terrific chicken curry!"

"Sold. Let's go find us a chicken."

As they started out of the restaurant, Emelina felt the curious stares drilling into Julian once more, and this time an unreasoning defensiveness took hold of her emotions. Damn it, whatever Julian was, it didn't concern these people! What right did they have to talk about him behind his back and eye him so rudely?

Pinning the nearest offender with a narrowed, challenging gaze, Emelina took a step closer to Julian and slid her arm under his. The small gesture couldn't possibly have been lost on the villagers. Emelina was definitely signaling where her alliance lay. Her chin lifted defiantly.

Julian glanced at her arm in surprise before crushing it against his side with a suddenness that suggested he was afraid she'd change her mind. Thus entwined, they made their exit from the cafe.

They walked in thoughtful silence up the street to the grocery store. Emelina didn't know how to ask for her arm back, and Julian appeared to have no intention of releasing it voluntarily.

Emelina could have cheerfully kicked herself. Why had she followed the impulse to take a stupid stand like this in front of the people in the cafe? Julian Colter didn't need anyone's assistance. He was the last one to be concerned about what the others thought!

"I'll have the butcher bone some chicken breasts," Julian offered as they entered the store at the end of the block.

"Okay, I'll see if they carry anything as exotic as chutney here," Emelina said quickly, grateful for the release of her arm. "Meet you at the checkout counter." She hurried down a far aisle, seeking a momentary escape more than she sought chutney.

It was something of an accident that she stumbled into a small row of bottles full of the spicy condiment at the end of the aisle. Perhaps it was some sort of strange omen, she decided, picking up a bottle and heading for the spice rack nearby to search for curry powder.

What she discovered at the spice rack, however,

was the middle-aged woman who, along with her husband, owned the grocery store.

"Oh, good morning, Emelina. I saw you come into the store a few minutes ago."

Emelina eyed the almost militant look in the older woman's eyes and cringed inwardly. Now what? "Good morning, Mrs. Johnston. How are you today? I'm looking for curry powder."

"Got some right here." Mildred Johnston reached for the small can and handed it to her. "Came in with that Julian Colter, didn't you?"

"Uh, yes, as a matter of fact, I did," Emelina mumbled, trying to back away. Mildred Johnston was an acknowledged source of prime information among the local gossips. Emelina had realized that much two days after she'd arrived in town and begun doing her grocery shopping at Johnston's Market.

"Heard you had coffee with him the other morning, too, dear," Mildred went on determinedly.

"Yes."

"You want to be careful about who you strike up a friendship with, Emelina. You don't know anything about Colter, do you?"

"Well..."

Mildred leaned closer. "They say he's in the Syndicate."

"Really?" Emelina asked weakly.

"If I were you, dear, I wouldn't get too friendly with him," Mildred Johnston murmured knowingly. "Bad news. Oh, he's kind of interesting, I'll grant you that, but a nice young woman such as yourself wouldn't want to get involved with someone in the Mob! Why, his name isn't even Colter!"

"It isn't?" Emelina felt the same stirring of rebellion she'd experienced a few minutes earlier in the coffee shop.

"I doubt it. Colter is probably an alias. He's hiding out while things cool down back east, you see. Take my advice, Emelina. Steer clear of him." Mildred concluded her small lecture with an admonishing nod.

The words came out before Emelina could stop them. "Mrs. Johnston," she began icily, "if I ever decide I need your advice concerning my friends, I'll ask for it. For your information, Julian Colter is a friend of mine. We're working together on a project and I trust him implicitly. At least I know he's not going to gossip about me behind my back and that's more than I can say for ninety-five percent of the rest of this town! Furthermore, I am not a nice *young* woman, I'm thirty-one years old. Old enough to make up my own mind about who I will have for a *friend.* You might want to take into consideration one other thing, Mrs. Johnston. If you're so convinced Julian is Mafia, you probably ought to guard your tongue, hadn't you? He might grow a little impatient with small-town gossip. And there's no telling how he might decide to put an end to it!" Emelina finished with relish.

Mildred Johnston stared at her, stunned. "You don't think he'd...he'd..." She began awkwardly, only to let the horrified sentence trail off as her gaze went past Emelina to the man who had appeared from the next aisle and was now standing behind her.

Emelina whipped around in time to see Julian smiling blandly at a stricken Mrs. Johnston. "Oh, there you are, Julian. Did you get the chicken? I have everything else we need except for the flaked coconut. I think it's toward the front of the store. Shall we go?" Head high, she led the way toward the checkout counter. Julian obediently followed, leaving Mildred Johnston staring.

He didn't say anything at all until he picked up the paper bag full of groceries from a very silent clerk and left the store with Emelina. Then he murmured quietly, "Throwing your weight around a bit with the locals, Emelina?"

She heard the amusement in his voice and glowered. "It was your weight I was throwing around. I don't like the way people stare and gossip about you, Julian. But I think Mildred Johnston will be a little more careful what she says from now on!" she concluded in grim satisfaction.

"I doubt it," he chuckled. "Although she may be a little more careful who she says it to. You can be quite intimidating, Emmy."

"She deserved it."

"Now it's you and me against the world, hmmm?" he questioned lightly as he led her into the post office building.

Emelina contented herself with anxiously chewing on her lower lip. Was that the way matters were shaping up between her and Julian? She had the distinct impression that she was edging over an invisible line which, if she crossed it completely, would somehow place her squarely in Julian's camp. If she wasn't very careful, she would find herself committed to more than just repaying a debt. It was a sobering thought.

The package that awaited her in the post office was even more sobering, however, although Emelina accepted it with the sigh of resignation with which she had greeted a lot of other packages just like it.

"From New York?" Julian inquired curiously, glancing at the return address label. "From a publisher?"

"A rejected manuscript," Emelina muttered, collecting it and the rest of her mail. "I'm used to them."

Julian's brow furrowed. "What will you do with it now?"

"Send it out to another publisher," she groaned as they started down the post office steps.

There was a pause and then Julian asked gently, "May I read it first?"

Emelina shook her head vigorously. "Absolutely not! No one reads my manuscripts except faceless editors in New York who send impersonal rejection notices! I don't even allow Keith to read my work! I have a policy of not showing my manuscripts to anyone who's not in a position to buy them."

"You're afraid of a face-to-face discussion about your work?"

"Terrified of it," she agreed firmly. "It's much too personal at this point. I can't explain it. I just know I haven't got the courage to allow anyone to read my work. Maybe I'm afraid they'll laugh or tell me I'm wasting my time. Or maybe I'm afraid they'll lie and tell me it's good when it really isn't. I only know it would be a waste of time, because I intend to keep trying to write, anyway. So why subject myself to unwanted criticism?''

''I see your point,'' he agreed slowly. ''But I'd still like to read something you've written.''

''Not a chance,'' she informed him brusquely. ''What time shall I come by for dinner tonight, Julian?''

''You do have a way of changing the subject, don't you?''

''Six o'clock?'' she prompted determinedly.

''That will be fine. Why don't you come inside while I unpack these groceries now, though? You can say hello to Xerxes again. Did you have breakfast?''

''Oh, yes...and no, thanks, I don't think I want to see Xerxes again. I'll come by this evening, Julian.''

''I'd like you to come in now,'' he told her coolly. ''How about another cup of coffee?''

''That's quite all right, I really don't want any more, thanks.''

''I insist,'' he murmured, his gritty voice lowering to an even softer note. ''After all, we seem to be friends, now, right?''

''Julian, I want to get this manuscript ready to mail off again, and there were some chores I was going to do around the cottage....'' But he already had the cottage door open, and Xerxes was leaping outside to greet them both. Before Emelina knew what had happened, she was standing in Julian's kitchen, watching as he unpacked the grocery sack.

''I have some wine I brought with me,'' she ventured, deciding to be civil. "I'll bring it along tonight." Absently she patted Xerxes.

"Excellent." He nodded approvingly as he opened the refrigerator and placed the chicken on a shelf. "Emmy," he began as he drew the last item out of the paper bag, "about what happened this morning at the coffee shop and later in the grocery store..."

Emelina was bracing herself for a return to that awkward subject when she realized he had stopped talking and was staring thoughtfully into the brown paper bag. "What's the matter, Julian?"

"The receipt's in the bottom of the bag," he noted slowly.

"It usually is," she retorted in mild annoyance. Why should that matter?

"Yes," he agreed even more slowly, still looking into the sack, "it is. The receipt usually falls to the bottom of the bag and gets tossed out with it. Or folded up and stored in a closet," he added carefully.

Emelina's eyes narrowed. "Folded up and stored in a closet? You mean in a closet like the one down in Leighton's beach house?"

"Ummm." Slowly Julian crushed the paper bag in his hand, but not before he had withdrawn the receipt. "Receipts are dated, Emmy."

Emelina found herself gnawing on her lower lip as she locked eyes with a suddenly very serious-looking Julian. Her mind clicked quickly as her imagination took hold. "You mean that if we went through those paper bags stored in Leighton's closet we might find some dated receipts?"

"It's a possibility. And since those paper bags were

probably transporting groceries Leighton knew he'd need while he stayed at the cottage..."

"We might be able to see when he was last here?"

"If we had enough receipts," Julian observed quietly, "we might even be able to see if there were some sort of pattern to his visits. If they occurred on a regular basis. Want to go have a look this evening around sunset?"

Emelina's eyes sparkled with new excitement. "Why don't we go now? No one would notice!"

"Someone might," he contradicted firmly. "We'll go later when we stand a better chance of finding the coast clear!"

"Oh, Julian," she protested disgustedly.

"You wanted my professional expertise in this matter, remember? It's no good buying advice if you're not going to follow it. Sit down, Emmy, while I give you a lesson in how to make really first class coffee!"

Emelina's second adventure in breaking and entering, or *prying open* and entering, as she insisted on calling it, took place at dusk. This time she and Julian wasted no time before climbing through the window and heading for the hall closet where Eric Leighton had stored his paper bags.

It took only a few tries to demonstrate that Julian's idea had merit. There were receipts in the bottoms of several of the grocery sacks. Hastily they collected all they could find, refolded the bags and hurried back out the window.

"We're getting pretty good at this," Emelina noted

gleefully as she climbed the path ahead of Julian clutching a handful of grocery receipts.

"Thinking of giving up writing for a life of crime?"

"This is not exactly a crime, Julian! Leighton's the criminal, not us."

"Keep reminding me," he begged.

Instantly Emelina felt a bit contrite. Perhaps Julian did not like to think of his chosen profession while he was on vacation or hiding out. All kinds of businessmen needed time away from the job, she supposed. "I'm sorry I'm making you work while you're supposed to be on vacation, Julian," she said as they topped the rise and walked to the cottage.

"Don't worry about it. I'm going to be well paid for my efforts, remember?"

That kept her quiet all the way through the chicken curry, a salad and a bottle of Chablis. This time it was Julian who wished he'd kept his mouth shut. He much preferred her lively conversation, he realized unhappily as they cleared the table. He should have resisted the desire to remind her yet again of the debt that lay between them.

It was his own insecurity about being able to collect on that debt that prompted him to keep referring to it, he thought as he stoked the fire in the fireplace and poured out two brandies. Talk about a shot in the dark! The odds of learning anything useful from those receipts on the coffee table were pitifully bad. Of course, there were always those "inquiries" he planned to set in action soon.

"Let's see what we've got here," he said briskly,

seating himself on the rug in front of the hearth and spreading out the receipts. "You keep track of the dates I read off, okay?"

"Okay." Some of Emelina's enthusiasm returned as she contemplated the pile of papers on the floor in front of Julian. Eagerly she picked up a pad and pencil and began to jot down dates as he read them to her.

Julian was the more astonished of the two when a pattern did, indeed, begin to emerge. Emelina, he guessed, had been expecting an important finding, but he had been considerably more doubtful. The relief he experienced as the pattern began to come together was much more than he would have expected under the circumstances.

"I don't know yet what we can make of it or how much stock we should put in it, but there's definitely a similarity about all these dates. They all fall on or about the twenty-eighth of the month, don't they?" he said at last, scanning the notes Emelina had taken.

She nodded. "All at the end of the month. Julian, we're coming up on another month's end. Next Wednesday will be the twenty-eighth of this month!" Her hazel eyes were vivid with anticipation and excitement.

Julian glanced up and saw the glow in her blue green gaze and something in him hardened. "Is this what it takes to make you look at me like that?" he heard himself whisper harshly. "A few clues about Eric Leighton?"

He sensed her tremor of awareness and knew she realized how the atmosphere in the room had abruptly shifted from the excitement of a hunt for clues to the excitement of a far more sensual sort of hunt. It had happened so suddenly that she didn't know how to handle it. Julian was grimly aware of the fact that he wasn't feeling much like a gentleman tonight. He wanted her too badly to give her the time she needed to deal with the violent shift in the mood of the evening. Every masculine instinct he possessed was urging him to move quickly before she thought of a way to escape.

"Julian..." she began hesitantly, her fingers tightening on the pencil in her hand. "Julian, I don't think we should..." She broke off again, her teeth nibbling uncertainly on her lower lip.

"Come here and let me taste that sweet mouth," Julian rasped softly, reaching for her. "I'll be a lot gentler on it than you are!"

With a rising surge of anticipation and desire, he eased her onto her back against the old rug, sprawling across her rounded curves with aggressive delight. She felt so *good* beneath him. So warm and soft and exactly right.

Slowly, lingeringly, he lowered his mouth to sample the lower lip she had been abusing with her teeth. On a husky groan of need, he took the full, inviting shape of it delicately between his own teeth and nipped with sensual demand.

Beneath him he felt her body stir. Julian's carefully leashed passion began to flare into blazing life. How could he possibly stop himself tonight?

He wanted his sweet Emmy with every fiber of his being. Tonight he would see to it that their bargain was sealed on yet another level.

Five

Emelina felt as if she'd been inundated by the wave of masculine desire that swept over her. She'd known an unusual level of response the last time Julian had taken her in his arms, but tonight it was as if he were intent on overwhelming her senses, rather than testing them.

The fact that he was succeeding at the task was a measure of how far she had gone along the road to commitment, because Emelina knew herself well enough to know she could not allow a physical bonding without an emotional and mental sense of commitment.

But even as Julian's body sought to master hers, leaving her fewer and fewer options as the seconds ticked past, Emelina's head whirled with chaotic questions. How could she be feeling this kind of commitment to this kind of man? Whatever bond existed between them should extend no further than the tie of indebtedness. God knew that chain was going to be bad enough to live with! How could she even be tempted to explore the physical commitment?

Even as she lectured herself with fierce desperation, though, Emelina realized the questions were rapidly becoming academic. Something in her did not want to fight this man. Long-submerged feminine instincts urged her to please him, and she was woman enough to recognize that on some primitive level she actually wanted to add another link to the strange chain that bound them together.

It was wrong. Crazy, foolish and impossibly dangerous. Yet as Julian's teeth probed with exquisite tenderness along her lower lip, Emelina found herself remembering the odd desire to protect and defend him that had overcome her earlier that day. The sense of wariness she had always felt around him remained, but it was now tempered by the demands of the pact they had made. For better or worse she was on his side of the fence until the debt had been repaid.

"Emmy, you make my blood hot, do you know that, sweetheart? Just watching you these past few days has made me feel too warm, too restless, too much in need. I want you to know the same kinds of sensations. I want you to want me so badly you'll give yourself to me completely. Let me make love to you, sweet Emmy."

Let him make love to her? The question was how could she possibly stop him? Emelina moaned, the small sound lost in his mouth as he covered her lips completely with his own. She felt a delightful tingle of anticipation and marveled at it. Quite suddenly she didn't want to think about the ramifications of what she was doing. Her instincts cried out for the full commitment.

"Julian, oh, Julian," she breathed as he slowly freed her mouth to explore the line of her throat. Her palms lifted to curve around his shoulders, testing the strength there. She could feel the hardness in his body and knew the extent of his arousal. It was intoxicating.

"Your body was made for mine," he growled, burying his lips in her throat as he slowly found the first button of her shirt. "There's something just right about it. Full and round and soft and unbelievably sexy!"

"If that's a nice way of saying I'm plump," she managed shakily, "I think I resent it!" The soft banter amazed her. Could this really be her daring to tease at a time like this?

"It's a way of saying you're perfect. Just what I need," Julian contradicted and then he drove his tongue between her parted lips as he found the second button of her shirt.

Emelina was so fascinated by the sensual rhythm he created that she barely noticed the complete removal of her garment until Julian's palm moved lightly over her nipple. Then she gasped aloud and writhed against him, trying instinctively to get closer.

Julian muttered something low and urgent and roughly exciting as she moved beneath his touch. His body grew even heavier on hers, crushing her softness deeply into the faded rug.

Sensation piled on top of sensation, but the dominant one was Emelina's growing desire to give Julian what he seemed to crave. Her body cried out to satisfy. It cried out, too, with an unexpected wish to be satisfied. She stirred at the realization, pushing her breast more firmly into his hand. When his thumb stroked erotically around the budding nipple she sighed with pleasure.

"Julian, I should stop you. I know I should stop you. Why can't I?" she asked wonderingly.

"There's nothing you could do tonight to halt me. Don't think about it, Emmy. Don't even think about it," he repeated with masterful assurance. As if to reinforce his words, Julian transferred his mouth to the tips of her breasts, using his teeth there with the same delicate deliberation as he had used on her lip. Emelina trembled and her leg, which still lay free of his weight, flexed at the knee. It was as if all the nerves and muscles in her body were slowly tightening. The feeling was at once delicious and a little unnerving.

"Touch me, sweetheart," Julian growled hoarsely. "Please touch me."

How could she deny him? Emelina's fingers moved through his hair and down to the nape of his neck, slipping inside the collar. There she kneaded the smooth band of muscle, glorying in the tremor that went through him.

Provoked by her accomplishment to further daring, she flattened her palms against his chest and drew them down to the first button of his shirt. Julian lifted his weight from her far enough to allow Emelina to unbutton it. When her fingers became increasingly awkward, he grew ruefully impatient and sat up to finish the task himself.

She lay on the rug looking up at him in the firelight and wondered at her own reactions. When Julian tossed the shirt aside and met her eyes, she immediately forgot the pulsing tautness in her own body and concentrated fully on his.

"You're so beautiful," she breathed, reaching out to lace her fingers through the crisp hair of his chest. "Like Xerxes."

His dark eyes burned over her as his mouth twisted in wry humor. "Like my dog? Thanks!"

"Sleek and strong and..." She broke off, not wanting to say the rest.

"And what?"

Emelina decided she ought to have guessed he would make her finish the sentence. "And a little frightening," she concluded honestly.

"Are you frightened of me, Emmy?" Slowly he stretched out beside her, his hand roving across her midsection to the fastening of her jeans. His gaze held her still as he began to remove the last of her garments.

"Sometimes." Her mouth had gone very dry, and her lower body felt too hot, too tense. What was wrong with her?

"Don't be. As long as I know I can trust you, you have no reason to fear me, sweet Emmy." He lowered his head and brushed her lips fleetingly. Then Julian slid his hands beneath the waistband of her jeans and pushed them down over her hips. Before Emelina could decide if she wanted matters to go that far, they already had. She lay nude on the hearth rug, her chestnut hair fanned out beneath her, hazel eyes watching him from beneath half-closed lashes.

In the firelight their bodies glowed almost golden. Emelina knew a fierce desire to see the rest of Julian's hard length. She wanted to see all of him painted with that golden glow.

"You're growing very bold," he teased gently as she found the zipper of his denims. "It's about time!"

Embarrassed, Emelina made to draw back her hand, but he caught her wrist and placed it firmly back where it had been. Encouraged, she slowly undressed him. The aggressive, aroused state of his body made her suck in her breath.

"Now touch me some more," he begged. "God, your fingers feel good on my skin!" All the while he stroked her thigh, weaving patterns on the soft curve that seemed to heighten the gathering tension in her. When he moved those patterns to the inside of her leg she moaned aloud and buried her face against his shoulder.

"Do you like that, Emmy?" he whispered, working his hand upward along the satin softness of her inner thigh. "Am I pleasing you, honey?"

"Oh, yes," she breathed and thought how kind he was to worry about whether or not he was pleasing her. Her ex-husband had never been overly concerned with the subject, assuming that if she didn't get whatever she needed out of the marital embrace, it was her own fault. Emelina found herself filled with such gratitude for Julian's concern that she wriggled closer on the rug and hesitantly reached down to feel the muscled slope of his leg. It was rough with hair and excitingly different from her own.

She tried to please him the way he was pleasing her, stroking and caressing closer and closer to the waiting hardness of him. But when she hesitated too long to take him intimately into her hand, Julian groaned and pushed himself against her palm, demanding the sensual touch.

As if the feel of her hands on his aroused body was something he had been anticipating for a very long time, Julian pressed himself closer. He slid his palm between Emelina's legs and under her rounded buttocks, using his thumb with erotic sensitivity on the flowering heart of her desire. Emelina was put totally off balance by the exquisitely erotic sensations that flooded through her limbs.

"Julian! Oh, my God, Julian! I feel so...so..." She couldn't find the words. The sensation was pleasurable, but it was also distracting. She forgot her wish to caress him as perfectly as he was caressing her. Emelina forgot everything for a moment except the warm, melting honey that was coursing in her veins. She wanted more of it; wanted to follow the path that beckoned as it never had before in her life. Nothing mattered now except learning at last what real satisfaction could mean.

Blindly Emelina groped for Julian's shoulders, tugging him close. Her legs separated invitingly and the hard tips of her breasts taunted him.

"Emmy," he rasped, obeying her feminine summons. "Emmy, I want you so!"

He shifted, raising himself over her. With a surge of power Julian fit himself between her thighs, entering the moist satin folds of her with a blunt impact that took away Emelina's breath.

The shock of his possession seemed to clear her mind for an instant, wiping out the strange, restless striving for satisfaction that had been driving her. As her body absorbed the solid strength of him Emelina came back to reality.

The important thing was to please Julian. She wanted that far more than she wanted to taste the ultimate passion. She wanted Julian to be happy.

When he nipped at her throat with gentle savagery and began to drive himself into her with a passionate cadence of growing desire, Emelina wrapped him tightly in her arms, arching her hips willingly to meet his.

"Yes, sweetheart," he grated fiercely, "give yourself to me. I need you so!"

Emelina obeyed, her whole being focused on satisfying him. She sensed that he wanted her to melt completely. Julian needed to know that she couldn't resist his lovemaking. Emelina bent all her energy on giving him what he sought. Her hands flattened against the planes of his back and her legs held him tightly as she clung to him, whispering the words she sensed he wanted to hear.

She tried to gauge the pace of his arousal, wanting to time herself perfectly for him. It was so important that he be satisfied! Aware of the steady hardening of his body and the muscled tension beneath her hands, she decided the moment had arrived for him.

Willingly, eager to provide exactly the response he wanted from her, Emelina threw herself into imitating what she felt must be a close semblance of the passionate convulsion that took hold of a woman at the completion of lovemaking. She sank her nails carefully into the firelit skin of his shoulders, tensed her lower body as tightly as possible and whispered his name over and over again in breathless abandon.

Emelina knew it must be an excellent reproduction of the real emotion because on the few occasions when she'd tried to please her ex-husband with it, he had been egotistically satisfied with the effect.

But instead of following her performance with his own genuine burst of masculine satisfaction, Julian went still above her. Emelina opened her eyes in confusion, aware of his hardness within her. What was wrong? she thought frantically. Wasn't he pleased? Why didn't he react the way men were supposed to react at times like this? Had she failed to satisfy him? Emelina knew a surge of fear at the thought. She had wanted so much for him to be satisfied!

"If you've finished with the theatrical performance, perhaps we could go on to the real thing?" In the firelight, Julian's features were drawn and taut with controlled passion and something else, something very close to anger.

All at once Emelina felt very vulnerable. He hadn't been fooled for an instant. Helplessly, hazel eyes wide and pleading, she looked up into his face. What could a woman say in a situation such as this?

"Julian…" She caught her breath, aware of the hard length of his frame covering hers so completely.

"Julian, I'm sorry. I can't. I mean, I never have been able to and I...I...only wanted to please you." The words came out in a sad little rush, and Julian's eyes blazed with dark fire.

"Shut up, my sweet Emmy and follow me."

His mouth came down on hers and his hips arched deliberately. Emelina gave up. She had done her best and had failed. Now she could only cling to him while he headed down strange paths that she had never fully investigated. She only hoped he wouldn't be too terribly disappointed if she failed to follow completely.

With the burden of trying to satisfy him off her mind, Emelina found herself concentrating on her own emotions. What were those flickering embers that were beginning to heat her loins and sent shivers down her spine? Where did this strange tension really lead?

Julian made love to her as if she were his whole world. He used his hands and his lips to tease and torment her as Emelina had never been teased and tormented before in her life. She abandoned herself to the incredible experience, no longer worrying about anything other than the thrilling pleasure that was rippling through her in waves.

She moved beneath him now, not with calculated thought, but with unconscious demand. Her nails sank into his skin again, but this time they nearly drew blood. Her legs wrapped him close, but this time she squeezed him with every ounce of her feminine strength, not fully appreciating just how strong she was.

"Julian!" The cry was a command and a plea as

Emelina's head arched backward over his arm and her eyes shut tightly against the invading desire.

"Hold me, Emmy. Hold me as if you'll never let me go!" Julian ordered roughly, his fingers sliding down between their bodies to find the tangled, moist thicket between her legs. There he did something that seemed to send Emelina over the edge of an invisible cliff.

In that final moment she couldn't even breathe his name. She had no breath left. The tension within her uncoiled in a flashing, electrical current of energy that convulsed every nerve and muscle in her body. She clung to the man above her as if he were the only refuge in the storm racking her soft frame. She was barely aware of the fierce unleashing of his own satisfaction. Dimly she heard her name being harshly called and then she collapsed beneath him, certain she would never be able to move again.

It was Julian who moved first, but not for some time. Emelina came drowsily out of her timeless, dreamless state as he reluctantly drew away from her body and rolled to one side. When she turned her head on the rug to look at him from beneath her heavy lashes she found him watching her with a grim satisfaction.

"Don't ever, ever lie to me, Emmy," he grated softly, moving his fingers absently through the chestnut brown tresses tangled around her head. "Not verbally or physically. You'll never get away with it. Trying to lie to me is the one sure way to make me very angry. I want only honesty from you, do you understand?"

In spite of the warm aftermath of pleasure, Emelina knew an abrupt shiver of chilling uncertainty. "I'm sorry, Julian. I only wanted to please you. I didn't think I was capable of...of finding out what it was really like and I knew you wouldn't be satisfied unless you thought you had pleased me so I...I tried to act pleased. Oh, I don't know how to explain," she mumbled, turning her head aside so that she no longer had to meet his eyes.

He caught her chin on the edge of his hand and raised her head again. This time she saw the tenderness in his eyes. "You sweet idiot. You're a creature of passion and excitement, don't you know that?"

"No," she retorted baldly. "I don't!"

"Well, you are and from now on I'm going to be the only man who has the right to put you in touch with that side of yourself. Is that very clear?" He traced the outline of her lips with his thumb.

Emelina felt too vulnerable and confused to argue. She could only stare at him, searching for an explanation of what was happening. Julian saw the grave questions in her face and leaned forward to brush his mouth against hers. "And if you ever pull a stunt like that fake act of passion again, I guarantee I will stop right where we are and turn you over my knee. By the time I've finished paddling your charming derriere you will be unable to think of playing any more games!"

Desperately she struggled for a way of responding to the indulgent gleam in his eyes. "That sounds kind of kinky."

His amusement exploded into outright laughter as

Julian gathered her close. "It is," he assured her. "Very kinky. I wouldn't dream of suggesting it if you weren't such a wild little witch in bed!" Then he drew his hand along her thigh and began teasing her mouth with his own. Emelina felt his amusement changing into another emotion.

"Julian?" she questioned softly as the first faint ripples of excitement began stirring in the pit of her stomach.

"You apparently have a lot to learn about making love, sweetheart, and considering your advancing age, I don't think we'd better waste any time."

"Oh," she said quickly, without pausing to think, "I've always heard that women are at their best as they go into their thirties."

"Show me," he invited.

When Emeline awoke the next time it was morning and she was lying in Julian's bed, not on the hearth rug. It wasn't the sunlight filtering through a cloudy sky that opened her eyes, nor was it another passionate advance from the man sprawled next to her. It was a cold, damp nose being thrust into her palm.

Xerxes watched her intently, his dark head resting on the bed. The expectant, faintly wistful expression on his face was enough to make Emelina groan and bury her own head back under a pillow.

Xerxes took more forceful action. He nudged her again with his nose and Emelina heard a tiny sound emanating from far back in his throat. Was Xerxes growling at her? That thought was enough to bring her wide awake. She stared at the dog suspiciously as she clutched the sheet to her naked breasts. As far as

Emelina was concerned, there was probably a great similarity between dog and master. She fully expected either one of them to resort to intimidation if they didn't achieve their objectives through more polite methods.

Xerxes looked up at her with a satisfied expression. He was making progress.

"He wants out," Julian yawned beside her. "It appears you've been elected for the duty. I can see there are some terrific fringe benefits to having you in my bed. Why don't you run along and let Xerxes out and then practice making coffee the way I showed you the other day?"

Emelina frowned severely into his blandly innocent face, a part of her far too aware of the fact that he was as naked as she was under the sheet. "I am not going to get into the habit of waiting on you and your dog!" Heaven help her! She wasn't going to get into the habit of waking up in his bed, either, she added grimly to herself. Even if doing so meant rediscovering a passionate side of her nature she hadn't dreamed existed. Some discoveries involved far too much risk.

Xerxes made that faintly menacing sound in the back of his throat again and Emelina snapped her head back to glare at him.

"I think you'd better get moving," Julian drawled behind her. "He sounds like he's getting impatient. And I could sure use that cup of coffee."

"I've told you, I'm not going to be a dogsbody for either of you!" she sniffed defiantly.

This time it was Julian who growled, a small, intimidating sound which belied the lazy humor in his dark eyes. Emelina wasn't up to dealing with two intimidating males on that particular morning. She snatched the quilt off the end of the bed and, wrapping it awkwardly around herself, stalked off to obey Xerxes's summons.

Julian watched her leave the room, his eyes following her with a curious mixture of amusement, remembered passion and possessiveness. Then he flung himself back against the pillows and contemplated his new future.

He would have to tread cautiously now. There was no doubt that he had rushed her into bed last night against his better judgment, but how could he have resisted staking the intimate claim? She was so exactly right for him, and Julian frankly acknowledged to himself that he had acted out of a very primitive fear of losing her. All his instincts bade him chain her as thoroughly as possible. And the bonds of passion seemed, to his male mind, yet another way of tying her to him.

His mouth curved slightly as he recalled the satisfying heat of Emelina's desire once it had been unleashed. Damn it, he really would paddle her nicely rounded rear end if she ever pulled that bit of fakery again! Her ex-husband must have been a complete fool to let her get away with that. He hadn't known what he was missing. Which was just as well, Julian assured himself complacently. He didn't want to think about the problems he would have encountered if he'd met Emelina and found her to be a happily married woman! She belonged to him.

Julian sighed and threw back the sheet, his bare feet hitting the wooden floor with a thud. He shook his head ruefully as he felt a twinge of desire just at the thought of Emmy Stratton in his arms. At his age he ought to have a little more self-control! With any other woman he would have had plenty of control, he realized as he headed toward the cold bathroom and switched on the electric wall heater. But Emmy was different. Emmy made him go a little crazy.

Which only made it all the more imperative that he employ some caution. The trap he was setting had to be as tight as possible. He didn't want to take any unnecessary risks.

Last night had probably been inevitable, Julian decided practically as he stepped under the shower. But he'd seen the wariness in her eyes this morning when she had awakened, and he knew that Emelina wasn't yet ready to agree to spend all her nights in his bed.

Which was only fair, Julian thought grimly. After all, he still had his side of the bargain to carry out.

"Here's your coffee. Take it or leave it," Emelina announced as she boldly walked into the bathroom and handed the mug around the edge of the curtain. Assign her to make coffee, would he?

The mug was taken from her hand but she wasn't given a chance to withdraw her fingers. Julian caught hold of her wrist and held her as he cautiously sipped the brew she had created.

"I don't think you were paying attention when I gave you that lesson," he finally declared consideringly. "This is pretty awful."

On the other side of the curtain Emelina smiled with defiant satisfaction. "I'm a slow learner."

"Not in every subject," he drawled, pushing aside the curtain to regard her as she stood still draped with the quilt. Her hair was tousled and she looked very inviting to his eyes. Deliberately he set down his coffee mug and used his free hand to unwrap her.

"Julian, no!" she protested, slapping at his fingers. Hastily she averted her eyes from his strong, naked length.

"Hush, sweetheart," he soothed in a deeply hypnotic growl. "I'm only going to help you get ready to face the new day." Gently he yanked her into the shower stall.

It was a long time later before Emelina sat down to breakfast across from Julian. Her mood was a precarious one, compounded of wariness and a feeling of commitment that made her deeply uneasy. A part of her wasn't at all sure she liked what had happened to her last night. It left her feeling strangely trapped. Another part of her was beginning to welcome the bonds closing in around her. That realization was the cause of her wariness. Being attracted to Julian Colter was frightening.

"About the dates on those receipts," Julian began calmly as he poured syrup over a stack of buckwheat pancakes.

"Yes, what are we going to do?" Emelina was more than a little grateful for the neutral topic.

"If there's anything to your crazy theory that Leighton is using his beach house for illegal activities, then we are led to the conclusion that those activities seem to be on a schedule. Whatever is happening is happening at the end of month.''

''That makes sense, doesn't it? Shipments of any kind, legal or illegal, normally get made on schedule.''

''Emmy,'' he sighed, ''I hope you realize how very unlikely it is that anything remotely resembling illegal activity will take place at that beach house next week.''

''We have to find out, Julian! This could be the break I've been looking for!''

''Okay, okay. We'll find out. I just want you to be prepared for disappointment,'' he advised steadily.

''I will be,'' she agreed too readily, not at all prepared for any such thing.

He looked at her. ''I also want you to remember that if I help you find out what is or is not going on at Leighton's cottage, I've completed my end of the bargain.''

Emelina swallowed an oversized bite of pancake and nodded mutely. ''You don't have to remind me,'' she finally managed in a small voice.

He groaned and reached across the table to cover her hand with his. ''I'm sorry, honey. I should have known I didn't have to remind you. After all, you always pay your debts, don't you?''

''Yes,'' she whispered and attacked her pancakes.

Julian allowed her to return to her own cottage after breakfast without an argument, which rather surprised Emelina. ''What are you going to do this morning?'' she found herself asking as she stood on his front step patting Xerxes good-bye.

"Make a couple of phone calls."

"To whom?"

"Someone who works for me. Run along, Emmy. I'll drop by for lunch. Don't bother trying to make me any coffee. I'll bring my own."

"Giving up so easily on training me?" she dared, smiling at him.

"Not at all. I just don't believe in trying to teach you too many things at once. I've decided to concentrate my energies in more productive areas at the moment. Areas in which you show a marked aptitude. We'll return to the coffee problem at a later date."

Emelina hurried down the steps and up the street to her cottage, her face warm and flushed under the impact of his too-knowing gaze. It was like falling into quicksand, this sensation of being bound more and more tightly to a man. She'd never experienced anything like it in her entire life, and she didn't know how to fight it.

Of all the men in the world, why did she have to find herself in this situation with someone like Julian Colter? Why couldn't she have found someone safe and traditional and nonthreatening?

Emelina tried to take a firm grip on her emotions as the morning passed. Somehow she was going to have to find a way to handle this crazy mess. It was bad enough that she was in debt to the man. She simply must not let the attraction she felt for him carry her over into the bottomless pit of love.

She happened to be glancing out the window an hour later when she saw Julian walk out of his cottage with Xerxes at his heels. Together they headed toward town. To find a phone booth? The summer cottages didn't have such amenities. Who was Julian going to call? Emelina shuddered to think of the sort of person one called in a situation like this! In an effort to take her mind off thoughts of Mafia henchmen she curled into a chair by the window and went to work on her latest plot. For some vague reason the hero she was describing began to take on marked similarities to Julian Colter.

Julian showed up as promised for lunch. He was carrying a thermos of coffee under his arm, and Xerxes tagged along at his side. The three of them ate in an atmosphere of comfortable familiarity, which amazed Emelina when she thought about it. But when Julian volunteered no information about the person or persons he had contacted that morning, she could contain her curiosity no longer.

"Well?" Emelina demanded, pouring out the thermos of coffee. "Did you get everything taken care of with that phone call?"

"Cardellini will be along this afternoon," Julian said mildly, lounging back in his chair.

"Who's Cardellini?"

"I told you. Someone who works for me."

"Yes, but what does he actually do for you?" Good lord! Why was she pressing the issue? Did she really want to know?

"He handles security matters for me," Julian explained gently. There was a cool gleam in his dark eyes that dared her to ask any more questions.

"I see," Emelina said weakly and concentrated on her coffee.

Cardellini did, indeed, arrive that afternoon. Emelina looked out her window, chewing nervously on her lower lip as the long black Lincoln Continental halted in front of Julian's cottage. A young, grim-faced man with dark hair and a pinstripe suit climbed out of the car and greeted Xerxes with a familiar pat on the head. Emelina could have sworn there was a faint bulge under the jacket to his suit, the sort of bulge made by a shoulder holster. Lovely, she thought unhappily. All her imaginings about Julian Colter's lifestyle were turning out to have a strong basis in reality.

She let the curtain fall back into place and lifted her chin with inner resolution. She had known what Julian was when she made the bargain. There was no sense letting herself get upset now. Her main goal was to stop Eric Leighton, and Julian Colter showed every sign of being able to handle the matter.

And if she was going to be a part of this, she might as well go the whole route, she added, grabbing her jacket from the closet and letting herself out the door. After all, she was *committed!*

Determinedly she paced down the street and up the steps to Julian's front door, where Xerxes greeted her cheerfully. The door, itself, however, was opened by the young man with the grim face, and Emelina had a moment's doubt as she stood looking at Julian's employee.

"I'm Emelina Stratton," she announced boldly.

"Let her in, Joe. That's the lady in charge of this little operation." Julian's voice came from the kitchen. "She's just in time to watch a professional make a perfect cup of coffee."

Joe Cardellini nodded gravely and stepped back. Emelina sidled hastily around him and glanced into the kitchen in search of Julian. "Hello, Julian, I just thought I'd drop by for a moment," she began quickly, watching as he measured coffee into a pot.

He cast her a sidelong glance. "You mean you thought you'd see how the plans were going, hmmm? Meet Joe Cardellini. He's the man who will get you your evidence, if there's any to be had."

Very politely Emelina shook the hand of the quiet young man in the pinstripe suit. She noticed that he was still wearing the jacket, and was grateful. It would have been difficult to carry on a normal conversation with a man wearing a gun in a shoulder holster. She'd rather not have to look at it.

"How do you do, Mr. Cardellini."

"Miss Stratton." He nodded formally. There was quiet reserve in young Joe's face. A reserve that spoke of a little too much of the wrong sort of experience, as far as Emelina was concerned. Then she realized that there was even more of that sort of look in Julian's features. How was it she was coming to overlook it in her lover's face?

Her lover. Hastily Emelina plunged into conversation. "What are you going to do down at the cottage, Joe?" she asked in what she hoped was a chatty fashion.

"Plant some listening devices and record whatever is going to happen next Wednesday or Thursday," he explained calmly.

"Oh." Emelina frowned and behind her Julian chuckled.

"What did you think he was going to do, lie in wait for Leighton on the beach and gun him down when he appeared next week? This is the modern age, Emmy. We do things scientifically, utilizing the best of modern technology. You want evidence? We'll get you evidence."

"Thank you," she mumbled humbly, not looking at either man.

"You're welcome," Julian drawled. He switched on the coffeepot before finishing his sentence. "The gunning down part will come later, if necessary."

Emelina flinched. "If necessary?" she squeaked.

"If we can't get sufficient evidence on Leighton to call him off your brother, we'll have to resort to other, more elemental techniques, won't we?" Julian smiled blandly.

Six

"Don't tease her, boss." It was Cardellini who responded first to Julian's outrageous words. "There's no need to go upsetting her like that. You'll just make her nervous." His serious gaze moved sympathetically over Emelina's taut face.

"She's been nervous around me from the start," Julian said dryly. "Don't worry about her, Joe. She knows what she's getting into. And so do I. Why don't you run along and take a look at the Leighton place."

"Yes, sir." Properly rebuked and sent about his business, Joe Cardellini quietly let himself outside.

Emelina's eyes narrowed. "He was only trying to be polite. You didn't have to dismiss him like a...a servant!"

"He works for me. For the salary that young man

receives he can take a few orders. How I treat him isn't his real problem, anyway."

"What is?" she demanded suspiciously.

"How you treat him is what will determine whether or not he gets to keep his cushy job."

Emelina's mouth fell open in astonishment. "How I treat him! I've only just met the man!"

"Ummm. And already he's leaping to your defense. Steer clear of him, Emmy, or I'll fire him." Julian calmly reached for two cups and saucers.

"That's utterly ridiculous and you know it! It's insane! What in the world is the matter with you?"

"I have this little problem with possessiveness. Want some good coffee?"

"No, thank you!" she flung back. "As Mr. Cardellini has observed, I'm already a little nervous. Getting more so by the minute, too!" She stalked to the window, giving him her back.

She didn't hear him cross the room, but suddenly he was standing very quietly behind her. When he reached around her to push a steaming mug into her fingers Emelina knew it was a peace offering, and she couldn't quite stifle the small smile that tugged at her expressive mouth.

"Are you laughing at me?" he asked, his lips against her hair.

She shook her head. "It's just that you remind me so much of Xerxes on occasion. When you put that coffee cup in my hand it reminded me of the way Xerxes shoves his head under my palm when he wants to be petted." She shook her head ruefully. "What am I going to do with the two of you?"

"Pet us." His fingers lifted to stroke the nape of her neck under the fall of chestnut hair and Emelina shivered.

"Are you trying to apologize for accusing me of seducing poor Joe?" she demanded, refusing to be placated.

"Maybe," he sighed. "I'm not used to apologizing, Emmy."

"Try it," she ordered succinctly.

She heard him draw in his breath before saying levelly, "I'm sorry, Emmy. I shouldn't have jumped down your throat like that for no reason."

"No, you shouldn't have," she agreed caustically.

"It's just that I'm a bit sensitive on the subject."

"You have no right to be!" she gasped, still staring out the window.

"You can say that? After last night?" The fingers at the nape of her neck moved caressingly. Emelina shifted restlessly, stepping just out of reach.

"What happened last night doesn't give you any rights, Julian," she whispered. Her fingers clenched into a small fist at her side as she realized that she was lying. Somehow it had given him rights. She didn't like it; didn't want to have to deal with it, but Emelina knew that the sensation of commitment she felt this morning was stronger than ever. She silently gritted her teeth and wondered if she'd gone out of her mind. Nobody but a lunatic would get involved in a mess like this!

"I don't think you really believe what you're saying, sweetheart. I think you know I'm not going to let you go to another man now that I've made you mine," Julian whispered heavily. "But you don't have to panic at this particular point. I'll try not to rush you."

"I can't tell you how that relieves my mind!" she snapped, spinning around to face him with one hand on her hip. Hazel eyes snapped fire as she glared at him. "I'll try to avoid a case of hysterics over the matter."

His eyes slitted briefly as he took a sip of his coffee. "Do that. I can't abide hysterical females."

"Choosy, aren't you?"

"Very. Now, having exhausted that argument, I suggest we go on to another topic. I was going to suggest we have dinner at a little restaurant up the coast tonight. We'll have to use your car, since I don't have one here."

"Are you going to include Joe in the invitation?" she demanded saucily.

"The issue doesn't arise. Joe will be gone by this afternoon. He won't be back until I call him back."

"And when will that be?" she challenged morosely.

"As soon as I think there might be something to hear on the tapes he's rigging up at Leighton's house. Now stop trying to provoke me, honey. We've got another four days to kill together before we see whether or not anything momentous is going to happen around the twenty-eighth."

"If you think I'm going to hang around so you won't perish of boredom..." she began seethingly, only to be interrupted as he took one step forward and removed the cup from her hand. The next thing

Emelina knew she was being soundly kissed. All the passionate memories of the previous night were re-awakened by that kiss, and it silenced her more effectively than anything else would have done. When Julian withdrew they were both breathing a little too quickly.

He rested his forehead lightly on hers and muttered huskily, "About tonight."

"Yes?"

"The invitation is only for dinner. Not bed."

Emelina didn't know whether to be relieved or disappointed. In the end relief won out. Or so she told herself.

She was still telling herself the same thing four days later on the twenty-eighth. Julian had been with her almost constantly, but he had made no further move to take her to bed. She went for long walks on the beach with him and Xerxes and occasionally into town for coffee and the mail. The trips into the village gave her some small satisfaction: the overt staring and low whispers had ceased. Word had apparently spread that Mr. Colter preferred not to be the subject of open speculation. And no one made any further move to warn Emelina that she was mixing with bad company.

"You've got them all terrorized, honey," Julian observed as they headed back to the cottage on the fourth day. "Notice how polite everyone was?"

"You mean you've got them all terrorized. All I did was point out the risk they were running. Julian, doesn't it bother you, having people talk about you like that?"

"Not particularly. I came here for rest and isolation. My reputation seems to have bought me a lot of both. Other than a few low-voiced remarks, no one has bothered me,'' he pointed out easily.

''Except me,'' Emelina noted dryly. ''I've really put a dent in your plans for rest and isolation, haven't I?''

''You,'' he said softly, ''have made the whole trip worthwhile.''

Emelina met the warm look in his eyes and took her courage in both hands.

''Julian, exactly why are you here in Oregon taking a vacation?'' She waited for the answer, her heart beating anxiously. Did she really want to hear that he was hiding out or that he was resting from the rigors of a Mob war? Worse than that, did she want to hear that he was a target for some competitor?

''I was trying to escape the pressures of business,'' he told her mildly.

Which told her absolutely nothing, she thought, and then decided she was grateful not to hear thc whole truth. Hastily she changed the subject. ''Well, today is the twenty-eighth, Julian. Maybe tonight we'll find out something incriminating about Eric Leighton,'' she said brightly.

''Maybe.''

''You sound skeptical.''

''Honey, I've told you from the start that this scheme of yours is nothing if not harebrained. It has the merit of being highly imaginative but...''

''But you don't think we're going to get anything useful out of it? Why did you go to all the trouble of having Joe set those hidden microphones, then?'' she asked.

''Because I always try to carry out my end of a bargain. Just as you do,'' he replied simply.

By the time Julian had walked Emelina back to her cottage later that evening there was still no sign of any activity around the Leighton beach house. Julian had allowed her a quick glance from the top of the bluff just to reassure her that she wasn't missing anything.

''Emmy, if anything at all happens down at that house tonight, we'll get it on tape. You're not to go near the place on your own, do you understand?'' he lectured firmly as they drew to a halt on her doorstep.

''I hear you, Julian,'' she sighed.

''Don't worry,'' he said with a lopsided grin, ''you're not going to miss anything. Just stay put until morning. And think about me,'' he added, pulling her into his arms.

Thinking about Julian Colter had occupied a major portion of her nights lately, Emelina decided in disgust as he released her after a quick, hard kiss. He had been as good as his word. There had been no attempt to rush her back into bed since their one night together. Emelina wondered at his patience, but she didn't dare question it aloud. Besides, if she were going to question anyone's motives, it should be her own! She was the one who seemed to be bothered by a curiously incomplete feeling as she lay alone in her bed at night.

Relieved, damn it! That was what she was, *relieved,* not lonely!

Xerxes nudged her for a farewell pat and then Emelina watched the two lethal-looking males walk back down the road. Was Julian right? Would tonight prove nothing? What would she do then? She had been counting so much on her wild plan bearing fruit. If this didn't work out, another way would have to be found to protect Keith.

Julian seemed willing to go the next step for her. With a faint shudder, Emelina let the curtain drop back into place and headed for bed. She'd think about alternatives only if her initial scheme didn't work. No sense borrowing trouble. She was far enough in debt as it was.

That thought kept her awake for the next two hours. Being in debt to a man like Julian Colter would be enough to keep anyone awake, she finally decided, tossing back the covers with a restless movement and padding out into the kitchen to see what might be in the refrigerator.

There was enough moonlight to make it unnecessary to turn on the kitchen light, so Emelina was standing in the dark, munching on a cracker spread with cream cheese when she saw the taillights of a car in the distance.

Someone was driving toward the beach. To be specific, someone was driving toward Eric Leighton's beach house. The remainder of the cracker and cream cheese went down awkwardly as adrenalin began flowing through her veins. Something was going to happen tonight after all! She had been right!

Hastily she choked down the cracker and sped to the bedroom to find her jeans. Dressing in the dark she yanked on a pair of tennis shoes, the denims and the black pullover sweater she'd worn the night Julian had discovered her at the Leighton cottage. She had to know what was happening.

Julian's warning not to go near the place was brushed aside as Emelina let herself out the front door of her cottage and started toward the bluff. The excitement of knowing her plan was working pushed everything else out of her mind.

Sticking to the shadows of the silent cottages, Emelina slipped along the street until she was hurrying past Julian's house. For a moment she was afraid she would hear Xerxes's familiar greeting, but all was quiet in the moonlight. The lights were out in the house as she went past.

At the edge of the bluff she lowered herself onto her stomach and wriggled closer to peer down at the beach below. She had been right. The car she had spotted earlier was taking the long way down to the house, following the graveled road that came from the far end of the beach. Shivering with the cold of the damp night air, Emelina watched with her heart in her throat. Would Eric Leighton be in that car?

The vehicle pulled to a halt in back of the cottage and a man about the age of her brother climbed out. Emelina stared, trying to remember exactly what Leighton looked like. It had to be he. Who else would possibly be arriving at this place at this time of night? The man was carrying a paper sack in one hand and a suitcase in the other.

Frustrated at being unable to ascertain what was happening, Emelina inched forward along the bluff.

If she were very careful, she could crawl unseen down the path once the man below had disappeared inside the cottage. When the door closed behind him and a light came on inside the old house she took a deep breath and, crouching low, began to edge down the bluff to the beach.

What could be going on down there? Why wasn't anyone else around? What was in the suitcase? The questions nagged at Emelina all the way to the foot of the bluff where she sought cover behind a rocky outcropping. She was lucky the stretch of beach was not open and sandy with no cover. The rocks along the edge of the cliff provided plenty of shelter.

But being closer wasn't providing any answers. No one else arrived and nothing at all seemed to be happening in the beach house. Emelina risked crawling across an unprotected stretch of ground to get to a larger rock that was nearer the house.

There she huddled, running her hands up and down her arms in an effort to ward off the cold while she surveyed the beach cottage. Why the devil hadn't she thought to fling on a jacket? She was going to freeze if she had to wait very long.

That thought had just flickered through her mind when the faintest of sounds behind her made her forget completely about the chill in the air. Instinctively she whirled, knowing there was someone in the shadows.

She moved too slowly. Before she could turn halfway, a hard palm was slapped across her mouth and Emelina was being borne down into the sand at the base of the rock. A man sprawled across her, his arms holding her securely.

"Shut up and stop struggling, you little fool!" Julian's voice was a fierce, grating whisper of sound in her ear.

Instantly Emelina went still, largely out of sheer relief. Carefully Julian removed his hand and sat up slowly, pulling her back against him. "Don't make a sound," he murmured.

Emelina struggled for the breath that had been knocked out of her, nodding mutely. The warmth of his body was very welcome and she huddled close. With one arm wrapped around her, Julian edged toward the side of the protective rock and glanced toward the house.

"Damn!" The single word was uttered with quiet force. "We're trapped here now. There's a boat coming in to shore."

Emelina tried to peek around the corner of the rock. "A boat?"

"Hush. I mean it, Emmy. Not a word out of you until we're safe back at my cottage. Believe me, I'll give you reason enough to yell then! I told you not to come down here tonight! How did you dare to disobey me like this? My God, woman, I'm going to wear the hide off your sweet butt with my belt!"

When Emelina started to protest he clapped his hand over her mouth again and ordered her to be silent. Damn it, she thought furiously, who the hell did he think he was? This was all her idea. Her plan, her scheme, not his! She had a right to follow the action.

Above her, Julian swore soundlessly and inched her

close to the cold sand, half covering her with his warmth. From Emelina's point of view, however, things had improved. She now had a partially obstructed view of the beach. There was a boat being rowed in to shore and Eric Leighton—it *had* to be Leighton—was casually walking down the steps of the cottage to meet the two figures who sat in the boat.

As soon as the small craft was beached, all three figures started back toward the house. Emelina caught traces of the low-voiced conversation as they passed within several feet of the rock behind which she and Julian were hiding.

"Geez, it's cold out here tonight. You got some coffee, Leighton?"

"Yeah, I picked some up on the way. You always complain about the cold, Dan. Even during the middle of summer, you bitch about it!"

"Ah, well," the third man opined philosophically, "considering the profit involved in these little trips, I, for one, am willing to get a little chilled while making the run."

"Everything on schedule?" Leighton asked crisply.

"Oh, yeah. Charlie's sitting out on the cruiser tonight, waiting for us to get back with the shipment."

"Charlie? What happened to the usual guy?" Emelina could hear Leighton's concern.

"Got picked up for indulging in a joint at a gay bar last week." The man gave a crack of laughter. "Can you believe it? Two years of running the hard stuff up and down this coast without a hitch and the poor joker gets busted for grass!"

"The cops were probably looking for an excuse to close down the bar he was in and he had the bad luck to be there on the wrong night," the second man decided. "It's okay, though. He'll be back on the run next month."

The remainder of the conversation was lost as the three men moved up the rickety porch steps and into the cottage. After what seemed an eternity Emelina dared to wriggle a little beneath Julian's enveloping weight.

"You're heavy," she whispered.

"Tough. Lie still."

"But they're inside the house now. They can't possibly see us."

"We have no way of knowing how long they'll stay there. We could be halfway up the path when they decide to head back for the beach. We'd be sitting ducks." Julian shifted slightly, drawing her more closely to him. "We're stuck here for the duration. I swear, Emelina, when this is all over I'm going to take measures to make sure you can't sit down comfortably for a week!"

"You're overreacting," she accused.

"I'm being amazingly calm under the circumstances! When I woke up and realized Xerxes was pacing the house, whimpering to get out, I knew something was wrong. I got dressed and went over to your place. As soon as I realized you weren't there I knew where to come looking." His hand on her waist tightened menacingly. "I just want you to know,

Emmy Stratton, that what I'm going to do to you when we get out of this mess will undoubtedly hurt you a great deal more than it does me!"

"You can just stop threatening me," she grumbled furiously. "No one asked you to come looking. I was doing fine on my own down here."

Above her she heard a strangled oath as Julian fought to control his temper. Before he could say anything coherent, however, the door to Leighton's cottage opened again and the three men emerged. The two who were heading for the small boat were still sipping coffee from paper cups, and one of them carried the suitcase Leighton had brought with him.

"Take it easy," Leighton said casually. "I'll see you next month."

The other two nodded, and a few minutes later Leighton was giving the boat a shove to wrench it free of the sand. He stood watching as the small craft disappeared around a jutting cliff and then he walked quickly back toward the cottage. A few minutes later the lights inside the house were turned off and Leighton was in his car, driving back up the road to the top of the bluff.

"Okay, Miss Secret Agent of the Year, let's go." Julian heaved himself to his feet, locking his fingers around one of Emelina's wrists. She was yanked up beside him and led toward the narrow path without a word.

It wasn't until they reached the top of the bluff that Emelina managed to catch her breath. Then she broke into excited speech, her face aglow with the triumph she was feeling. "It worked, Julian! We know for certain now that Leighton's using the cottage for drug dealing or something. I can't wait to tell Keith. All he'll have to do is confront Eric with the facts and the man won't dare try to continue blackmailing him. What Keith has on Leighton will be a lot more dangerous than what Leighton has on my brother!"

"You think it's going to be that easy?" Julian growled roughly as he hauled her toward the cottage. "You think a man like Eric Leighton is going to tolerate the fact that your brother has an idea of what's going on once a month down there on that beach? You're a fool, lady. If your brother tries to reverse the blackmail, he's very liable to wind up very dead!"

The blood drained from Emelina's features. When Julian stepped inside the door and turned on the light, it was to see a very stricken woman staring back at him. Her hazel eyes wide with sudden fear, she stood stock still in the middle of the cottage living room.

Ruthlessly he shoved aside the urge to enclose her in his arms and offer comfort. "It's about time you had a healthy dose of fear," he rasped, shoving his hands into his jeans pockets and planting his feet wide apart as he confronted her implacably. "This isn't a game, Emmy. I'll admit I was surprised to see Leighton actually make an appearance down there tonight. I'll give you full marks for your intuition and your imagination. But you get a big zip for intelligent reasoning. You could have gotten yourself in a hell of a lot of trouble out there on that beach. What do you think Leighton and his friends would have done if they'd discovered you?"

"I was very careful, Julian!"

"You were very stupid," he corrected grimly.

"Stop yelling at me, Julian! It was my plan. I had every right to see if it was working!"

"I gave you orders to stay away from that house tonight. You gave me your word on the matter."

"I did not," she flared. "You asked me if I understood your orders and I said I did. I didn't promise to obey them."

"You've got a hell of a lot of nerve splitting hairs like that," he snapped.

Emelina blinked, beginning to realize just how angry he really was. Her teeth sank unconsciously into her lower lip as she began looking for ways to placate the devil. "Look, Julian, I'm sorry you were so worried, but everything worked out all right. There was no harm done, and we know now that Leighton really is up to something on the twenty-eighth of each month. I really appreciate your help in setting up my trap, and that was a positive brainstorm you had regarding the receipts in the bottom of the grocery bags. Without that clue we might have wasted weeks of watching and waiting. But there's no need to be so angry now. Everything is fine. We're on top of the situation at last, and Keith and I can take it from here."

He stared at her incredulously. "Forget it, Emmy. You're not going to soothe me the way you would Xerxes, with soft words and a few pats on the head!"

The dog in question lifted his ears inquiringly as he watched the two humans across the room. When they continued to ignore him, however, he went back to dozing quietly.

"I'm not trying to soothe you," Emelina stormed. "I'm trying to reason with you!"

"I'm not in a mood to listen to your convoluted reasoning. I'm in a mood to paddle the daylights out of you. It seems like the only way to make my point this evening!"

Emelina took an instinctive step backward, abruptly aware of how close he was to carrying out his threat. "Julian, don't you dare touch me!"

He took a purposeful step forward. "Don't you know better than to dare the devil, Emmy?" he drawled with heavy menace. "I'm damn well going to touch you. I'm going to teach you a lesson you won't soon forget, lady. From now on, when I give you an order you're going to obey it."

Emelina's nerve broke. There were times in a woman's life when discretion truly was the better part of valor.

Emelina turned and fled through the front door of the cottage, wrenching it open and sailing over the threshold before she even stopped to think. Through the open door behind her Xerxes bounded happily, more than willing to participate in this new game, even if it was nearly one o'clock in the morning. After him came Julian.

Run from him, would she? Julian thought furiously as he leaped down the steps in pursuit. Didn't she realize she belonged to him now? If he wanted to chew her out for disobeying his orders, he damn well would do exactly that! If he wanted to rage at her for scaring him senseless, he had every right! She had come close to getting herself killed, and she deserved to pay for the hell she had put him through.

He saw her run up the street toward her cottage, Xerxes dancing at her heels. In the moonlight Emelina's hair flew out behind her, and her rounded flanks seemed to taunt him. Julian realized he wanted to do a hell of a lot more than pound that sexy bottom of hers. After he'd driven home the lesson he intended to teach her, he wanted to make love to Emelina until she cried out for mercy. Let her run. It would only make the final reckoning all the more gratifying.

Steadily he closed the distance between them, grimly aware that the chase was sending a surge of pure masculine heat through his veins. There was something primitive and satisfying about running down one's woman in the moonlight, Julian acknowledged. The elemental chase cut through all the layers of civilization and put matters on a very basic level. He felt strangely exhilarated and fiercely determined to win thc contest of wills.

Then he was upon her. She made a small, half-strangled sound of protest as his arm closed around her waist and dragged her to a halt in the middle of the road. Xerxes paused, glancing up questioningly. Was the game over already?

"Julian!" Emelina gasped, struggling for air. "Let me go! Put me down this instant!"

He ignored her demand, spinning her around instead and stooping briefly to throw her across his shoulder. He was aware of her confusion and disorientation as she desperately tried to catch her breath. Julian locked her firmly in place, aware of the full curve of her thigh under his hand. It was rapidly becoming a toss-up as to which he would do first: turn her over his knee or make love to her. He contemplated the two alternatives all the way back to the cottage.

Emelina experienced a combination of outrage and fear that left her as breathless as the short, panicked run. Desperately she doubled her small hand into a fist and pounded fruitlessly on his back. He seemed utterly impervious to the assault. When she tried to struggle, he slapped her smartly across her derriere.

"You might as well settle down and behave yourself because you're not going to get free," Julian growled as he mounted the steps to his cottage and kicked open the door.

Something about the way he used his booted foot on the door brought home to Emelina just what state of mind Julian was in. The masculine aggression in him was very evident. He was aroused, both with anger and with another emotion. She swallowed uneasily and realized just how highly charged the situation really was.

Julian didn't pause as he carried her over the threshold. Without hesitation he strode down the short hall to the bedroom. Bending, he dumped Emelina unceremoniously into the center of the old bed. As she sprawled there, he straightened, his hands on his hips, and stood surveying his captive with satisfaction and anticipation.

Emelina watched him with grave uncertainty. She was still outraged at his actions, but she vaguely realized that she wasn't exactly afraid of him. At least, not in the literal sense. Julian Colter was aroused and affronted and highly displeased with her this evening, but she knew with sure feminine instinct that he wouldn't ever hurt her in any serious way. She had known that from the moment he had caught up with her and tossed her over his shoulder. Even in his aggressive mood, there had been a certain care about the way he had handled her. A man intent on physically hurting a woman would not have touched her the way Julian had.

All of which did not mean that the next few minutes were going to be very comfortable. There was no escaping the fact that Julian was far from being placated.

"Please, Julian, try to calm down and be reasonable," she began carefully, scooting backward across the old bedspread. "I'm sorry I annoyed you tonight, but if you'll just take a moment to think it out, you'll realize I had every right to keep an eye on Leighton's place this evening."

He contemplated her with narrowed eyes as he raised his fingers and coolly began undoing the buttons of his flannel shirt. "I've been asking myself all the way back to the cottage whether I ought to beat you or make love to you until you can't move. I think I've finally made up my mind."

Emelina's eyes widened nervously, and she inched a little farther toward the opposite side of the bed. The direction in which she was retreating was a dead end, however, because the bed was shoved up against the wall on the far side.

"Julian, this is a time for talk. S-sex isn't an answer

in a situation like this,'' she tried to say rationally. ''We have a—a slight misunderstanding between us, I'll grant you. I can certainly see your point of view,'' she added quickly as he slung his shirt across the room and dropped his hands to the fastening of his jeans. Then she drew in her breath sharply as he kicked off his shoes and stepped out of the denims. In a few short seconds he was totally naked. She could only stare in stricken fascination at his aroused and predatory body.

''Come here, Emmy,'' he commanded far too softly. ''Come here and tell me about our slight misunderstanding. Let me make my point of view even clearer.''

Her eyes moved helplessly across the dark, curling hair of his chest, down to the strength in his thighs before she tried once more to meet his gleaming eyes.

''Julian, sex never solves anything!'' she squeaked.

''I disagree,'' he murmured, putting one knee on the bed. ''I think it's going to afford me a great deal of satisfaction. And if it doesn't, I can still try my other alternative.''

''Beating me? Julian, you wouldn't dare!''

He merely smiled. It was the sort of smile she could imagine Xerxes giving a victim before he launched himself for the *coup de grace.* In that moment Emelina knew that she didn't stand a chance of deflecting Julian from his intent.

''Come here, my sweet Emmy,'' he growled huskily. ''I'm going to ride you tonight until you don't have the energy left to try running from me again.''

Emelina sucked in her breath and scrambled out of

reach until she was up against the wall, figuratively and literally. "Damn it, Julian, I won't let you intimidate me!"

He didn't bother with any more words. Julian's dark eyes went almost black as he reached for his woman with the determined arrogance of a man who intends to take what belongs to him.

Seven

It was Emelina's ankles that Julian grabbed. He manacled them with an unshakable grip that was surprisingly gentle and then he tugged her toward him across the bed. As he pulled her close he used his grip on her slender ankles to part her legs until she was lying helplessly sprawled before him. Kneeling between her jeans-clad thighs, Julian looked down at her with lambent fire in his eyes.

"Did you think I'd let you get away from me, sweetheart?" Slowly, with infinite promise, he lowered himself along the length of her. His fiercely masculine nakedness burned through the fabric of her clothing as he let her know the full weight of him.

Emelina tried to shift beneath the erotically crushing force of his body and found herself unable to move. He lay blatantly between her legs, framing her face with his rough palms. Emelina told herself she wasn't really afraid, just a little wary because of the aggressive way he had chased her down and hauled her back to the cottage.

"You can be awfully arrogant, Julian," she accused on a husky note. She watched his taut features from beneath half-lowered lashes, aware of the hardness of his legs as he stretched between her thighs. Her pulse, already quickened because of the chase, was now racing with the stirring of passion. "Arrogant and uncivilized."

"You bring out the primitive in me," he drawled, nuzzling the curve of her throat. "And if we're going to trade insults, I could make a few unflattering remarks about your brains, or lack thereof! Don't ever, ever take a chance like you did tonight. Do you hear me, Emmy?"

"It was my plan and my neck I was risking," she pointed out cautiously, wondering just how much she really meant to him. It occurred to her that his concern went beyond what she would have expected. How much did he truly care for her?

"Your pretty neck belongs to me, remember? I have first claim on it until you pay off your debt!"

Emelina's eyes widened in renewed outrage. "The *debt!* Is that all you're worried about? That I survive long enough to pay you? Why, you selfish bastard! If you think you can drag me into bed after making a statement like that, you're out of your mind!"

"Emmy, Emmy," he soothed on an astonishing note of indulgent humor. "You know damn well you're in my bed because I want you here and because I can make you want to be here. Forget about the debt for now and make love to me."

He silenced her further protests with a heavy, drugging kiss that merged the warmth of their mouths. He forced the intimate taste of himself on her until she was intoxicated with the essence of him. Julian continued to hold her face still for his kiss, while he anchored her body with his.

With an unconscious sigh of surrender, Emelina softened beneath him. This was the man who could unleash the passion within her. This was the man whose touch she had been craving for the past few days. Never before in her life had she truly craved the feel of a man's hands on her body. And this was the man she instinctively wanted to protect even though he was probably the last person on earth to need her poor defense.

Her fingers lifted to thread through the darkness of his silvered hair, and her legs closed restlessly around his naked thighs. Emelina knew in that moment that she was where she wanted to be. Why should she go on resisting the irresistible?

"Ah, Emmy, you're so warm and soft and perfect," Julian growled as he felt her response. "I would chase you across the face of the earth, let alone down a short street. I need you in my bed."

"Yes, Julian, oh, *yes!*" She squirmed beneath him as the tingling awareness in her loins began to escalate. His thrusting manhood was pressed sensually against her, and she longed to have him undress her completely. The passion which flared between them seemed to spring to life so easily! For her all it really took was his touch and the knowledge that he wanted her.

"Do you need me the same way?" he whispered provokingly. The tone of his deep voice told her he knew full well that she was rapidly becoming lost in the maze of physical response.

"Please, Julian."

"Tell me about it," he breathed as his fingers went to the hem of the black pullover and slipped underneath the fabric to find her breast. "I want to hear you say the words."

"I want you, Julian. You must know how much!" She trembled as he rasped her nipple gently with the palm of his hand, and her fingers raked along his bare shoulders.

"I want to hear you tell me exactly how much. What do you feel when I touch you like this?" he persisted, taking the budding tip of her breast between thumb and forefinger.

Emelina's head shifted restlessly on the bedspread, and her eyes closed tightly as the delicious sensations rippled through her body. "You make me *ache,* Julian. I never knew what it was like to really ache with need until I met you."

He groaned as she spoke the words with passionate honesty. Then he lifted her briefly against him and pulled the top over her head. Casting the garment onto the floor, Julian lowered her back down onto the bedspread and crushed her bare breasts with his chest. His eyes burned over her face as she sucked in air.

"Oh, my God, Julian..."

"I can feel your nipples," he breathed tightly.

"Like hard little berries pressing into me." Then he lowered himself along the length of her until he was tasting those same berries with his damp, velvet tongue.

When Emelina was beginning to think she would go mad from the tantalizing effects of his lovemaking he suddenly pulled away from her, moving back to a kneeling position between her legs. She opened her lashes slightly to find him watching her with passionate intensity.

"Julian?"

"Finish undressing yourself for me, honey," he commanded in a throaty growl. "Unfasten your jeans and take them off for me. I want to watch you as you get ready to go to bed with me."

Emelina hesitated, suddenly shy. She wasn't at all sure her fingers would function properly under the impact of that dark gaze. It was easier to let him take the initiative when it came to doing away with her clothing. To undress herself seemed yet another act of commitment; a gesture of acceptance.

But hadn't she already accepted him as a lover? What was the point of stalling now? Slowly her hands went to the fastening of her jeans.

"Don't stare at me so," she begged, her fingers trembling as they began to lower the zipper. "You're making me nervous!"

"You're making me a little crazy," he retorted, the corner of his mouth kicking upward as he moved back a bit to give her room. When she awkwardly slid the jeans to her ankles and let them drop off the edge of the bed Julian reached out to touch the vulnerable inside of her thigh with a feathering action that made her moan his name in soft pleading. Provocatively she held out her arms to him, urging him close once more.

"Your panties," he reminded her, letting his fingertips stray to the center of the scrap of nylon, which was all that remained of her clothing.

"You're a beast!" But already she was lifting her hips against his hand, wanting more of his touch.

"I'm only a man who wants you very badly. And I think you want me too. I can feel the hot mist of you, sweetheart. You're such a passionate little creature. My God, Emmy. Take off your panties for me!"

Under the impetus of that command, coupled as it was with the incredible desire in his eyes, Emelina, her fingers trembling more than ever, managed to remove the last of her clothing.

"My sweet Emmy." With a muttered, half-savage exclamation of need, Julian came back to her, sliding aggressively into the warmth that waited for him at the juncture of her soft thighs.

Emelina gasped aloud as he possessed her with the urgent force of a man who can wait no longer for his woman. She clung to him, seeking the hard strength he offered with undisguised need.

Slowly Julian set a heated rhythm that tautened the mysterious tension within her until Emelina thought she would burst. She listened to the arousing, exciting words he grated against the skin of her throat and in the throes of her hunger, whispered many of them back to him. They seemed to provoke him as much as they did her.

"Hold on tight, honey," he rasped as he sensed the

approaching rapids in the turbulent stream of their lovemaking. "Just hold tight and let it happen!"

Emelina gave herself up to the ecstasy he provided, unaware of the half-moons her nails left in his shoulders or of the way her thighs enclosed him so tightly he thought he might never be free. When she stiffened beneath him, Julian managed to raise his head far enough to watch the flow of emotions across her face. Then he was pulled into the torrent with her, unable to hold back any longer.

He watched her float back to reality in his arms, smoothing a strand of chestnut-colored hair back from her face as she opened her eyes to meet his gaze. "This is where you belong, Emmy. Here in my arms. Don't try to run away from me again. I'll only come after you."

"Will you, Julian?"

What was she thinking? Probably that he was incredibly arrogant to make such a statement. Julian sighed. She had no way of knowing how far he was prepared to go to make his words the truth. What would she say when he told her what he'd decided to demand as her part of their bargain? Would she argue and accuse and then agree because she was a woman who always paid her debts? Or would she try to run away rather than face the sentence he intended to impose?

No, thought Julian in deep satisfaction. She wouldn't run. She might be furious, perhaps even fiercely resentful of the situation in which she found herself, but his Emmy would pay her debt.

He could bank on it.

"You look very pleased with yourself, Julian Colter," she observed, arching one brow as she stared up at him from the curve of his arm.

"I am," he said simply, bending down to kiss the tip of her nose. "And it's all your fault."

"Is it?"

"Ummm. I always like it when I can make my point in such a satisfying manner." He grinned, the lazy pleasure in his eyes completely unhidden.

"You do it this way a lot?" she asked with an attempt at flippancy.

The grin was wiped from his face and replaced with a narrowed stare. "What do you think?"

For some reason Emelina found herself taking the question very seriously. "I don't think so," she said slowly. "I don't think you would use sex to control a woman. Not in the final analysis."

He regarded her interestedly. "Why not?"

"Because it's not a dependable weapon and you're sophisticated enough to realize it. You know that the loyalty and commitment you want from a woman can't be bought with sex."

"You're very philosophical this evening," he grated. "You're also right. I take great pleasure in being able to make you melt in my arms, but, unfortunately, I know you wouldn't obey me or stay with me or even spend any time with me just because you like what I can do for you in bed." He sounded disgusted at not being able to wield that particular weapon.

"You'd rather I'd promise to do anything you said just because you're good in bed?" she dared to tease.

"It would make things simpler."

"It would also make me a rather shallow creature. Someone at the mercy of her own passions," Emelina pointed out coolly.

"Instead of which, you are at the mercy of your own concept of integrity, aren't you?" he threw back enigmatically.

"What's that supposed to mean?"

He stroked her with slow intent. "Someday soon I will explain. Go to sleep, Emmy. In the morning we have to talk about what happens next."

Emelina yawned obediently, suddenly very tired. "About Leighton and his gang?"

"And about your brother. He has a right to know what's happening down here. What happens next should be up to him."

"You have a plan to suggest to him?" she queried sleepily.

"I'll tell you all about it in the morning." Tucking her into the shape of his body, Julian urged her wordlessly to sleep. But long after she had quieted in the curve of his arms he lay awake in the darkness, thinking about what she had said. Emelina was right. He knew better than to try to control her with sex. It would never work. Did she have any inkling of just how he did plan to control her? Probably not. As far as he could tell she hadn't thought beyond the present. Julian stared at the shadows on the ceiling and thought about the risk he was planning to take. He couldn't bear to contemplate the prospect of failure.

The first words Julian spoke to her the next morning took Emelina by surprise. She was dutifully hand-ing him a cup of coffee while he showered when he said, "We'll leave for Seattle this afternoon. As soon as Joe gets here and plays those tapes for us."

"Seattle! Today?"

"Emmy, I hate to tell you this, but your coffee is not improving. I don't think you're trying."

"Perhaps I haven't enough incentive to try harder." She grinned into the mirror as she ran his comb through her hair.

"I might have let you off the hook last night for disobeying me, but don't count on my overlooking your lack of effort in coffeemaking too long," he threatened. "This brew of yours really is a beating offense!"

"I hadn't noticed that you let me go scot-free last night," she complained, stretching her deliciously sore muscles. She was wearing his toweling robe and in the mirror she looked all soft and fluffy. Emelina had never thought of herself that way before, and she wasn't sure the notion pleased her now. Deliberately she grimaced into the steamy mirror, baring her teeth like Xerxes.

"What the hell are you doing? Making faces at yourself?"

She snapped her head around to find him watching her while he sipped the coffee. "I was trying to regain some of the feistiness that you crushed last night with your macho manners!"

He grinned his slashing pirate's grin. "With very little prompting I could be persuaded to carry you back into the bedroom and crush it some more. It springs back so nicely.''

''Is that a sexual innuendo?'' she demanded.

''Yeah. Want me to explain it to you?''

''No thanks. Tell me why we're going to Seattle,'' she ordered with a sniff of disdain.

''I want to talk to your brother.''

''Why, Julian?'' This time there was a serious note in her voice, and she turned to meet his gaze worriedly.

''I told you last night. He has a right to be consulted about what happens next. He's got a couple of alternatives.''

Emelina tapped the comb on the sink rim while she thought about that. ''I don't think so, Julian.''

He lifted one black brow in lazy inquiry. ''Emmy, you know as well as I do that you don't have the right to make this kind of decision for him,'' he said very gently.

''I know. I agree that it's up to Keith what he chooses to do next. He's the victim in this little mess. But I don't think I want you talking to him about the situation or offering him advice.'' She was beginning to feel a little nervous talking about such a serious subject while he stood gazing at her from the shower. She tried to explain. ''Julian, you promised this matter would be just between you and me.''

''You're chewing on your lower lip again, which means you're getting very anxious about something. I think I'm beginning to get the drift.'' His voice hardened. ''You're afraid I'll try to involve Keith in this bargain of yours?''

"Will you?"

"I gave you my word, Emmy. The only one I'll expect payment from is you." This time she could hear the thread of steel in his words.

"But if you go to Keith and he agrees to accept your help in finishing the matter," Emelina began breathlessly, "won't you—that is, will you consider him *involved?*"

"No. As far as I'm concerned it's all part of the same deal, Emmy."

She stared at him, eyes wide and anxious for a long moment, and then she nodded and turned away to finish her hair.

"Do you trust me, Emmy? Do you believe I'll keep this just between you and me?" he pressed, an underlying note of urgency in his question.

"Yes, Julian. I trust you." And she did. Given what she had read about Mafia dons, she didn't know why she should trust him, but she did. Emmy drew in a long breath and said conversationally, "When are you going to get out of the shower and fix us a pot of decent coffee?"

"I think we'll go into town for coffee this morning," he told her thoughtfully.

"Too lazy to make it yourself?"

"No, but I'm in the mood to watch you terrorize the townspeople."

"Julian!" She whipped around to stare at him as he ducked behind the plastic curtain.

"I love it when you get all protective in my defense," he drawled. "Makes me feel wanted. Between you and Xerxes I feel so *safe!*"

Emelina glowered ferociously at the shower curtain, but she couldn't think of anything to say. What really bothered her was that he was right. And it was all so ludicrous. The one thing this man definitely did not need from her was protection. He got all the protection he needed from men like Joe Cardellini who carried guns in shoulder holsters and looked at the world through grim eyes.

"We have to go into town anyway," Julian was saying conversationally. "I'll need to use the payphone at the store to call Joe."

Forty minutes later Emelina dug at the dust in the street with one toe while Julian stood inside the phone booth making his call. The black Lincoln was pulling up in front of the cottage an hour after that.

"Where did you drive from this morning, Joe?" Emelina asked interestedly. "You got here so quickly."

"Portland," he said, his gaze softening as he looked down at her. Emelina knew that that softening was as far as the expression would ever go. It was clear that Joe Cardellini would never dream of poaching on his master's preserves. Not because he stood in fear of Julian, Emelina realized with sudden insight, but because he respected his boss far too much to trespass. This morning Julian appeared to realize the same thing because, although he was as casually possessive as ever, there were no more veiled warnings either for her or for Joe.

"Have you been staying in Portland all this time?" she queried.

"I've been assigned there for the past couple of years," he explained politely.

"Assigned? Oh, I see." Emelina nodded wisely, remembering that the modern Mob was run like a cross between a closely held family corporation and the military. Julian's interests must extend far, indeed, to warrant having a "security" person stationed in the Northwest. The thought was depressing.

Sooner or later Julian would go back to "business" and this romantic idyll would come to an end. The next time she heard from Julian after this episode had ended would be when he called in the tab. Emelina stifled a shudder of gloomy dismay. Sooner or later the piper would have to be paid.

"Emmy? Are you listening?" Julian interrupted her thoughts, frowning briefly at her inattentiveness. "Joe's going down to Leighton's house to collect the mikes and then we'll listen to the tapes."

Emelina nodded and straightened her shoulders. This was what she had come for.

In the end the tapes proved every bit as incriminating as she could have wished. They confirmed and clarified the smatterings of conversation she and Julian had heard on the beach that night, portraying Eric Leighton and the others as a crew of professional drug smugglers who had been operating with impunity along the West Coast for nearly two years.

"I wonder why he bothered with something like blackmail. He's making money hand over fist with this stuff," Joe noted curiously. "Why risk the other?"

"Jealousy," Emelina sighed regretfully. Both men

looked at her and she explained. "I think Eric was simply jealous that my brother managed to make it in the establishment. Keith has acquired everything Eric wanted: respect, success, even a little power, and all legitimate. Eric was always envious of my brother, I think. Even when both were going through their radical stage it was Keith who had the respect and attention of their fellow radicals, not Eric. My brother is a natural leader," she concluded with a mild shrug.

Julian nodded slowly, accepting her explanation. Then he glanced at Joe. "Did you get everything out of the cottage?"

"There's not a sign of anything having been touched, boss. You ought to know I wouldn't leave any evidence." Joe fixed a reproachful expression on Julian's hard features.

Julian smiled. "I know. I'm just anxious to tie this thing up neatly."

Emelina hesitated, glancing from one man to the other as she chewed on her lower lip. "What we did by bugging the cottage—that was illegal, wasn't it?"

"Let's just say that I'm not going to turn that bit of evidence over to the Oregon police. That information was just for our own use to confirm your suspicions."

"The police!"

"Yes. If I can talk your brother into it, that's who we're going to turn this over to as soon as possible."

"But, Julian," she exclaimed, "you can't risk that. Neither can Keith!"

"Just let me handle it, okay, Emmy? Run along and get packed."

She argued with him in the back of the black Lincoln all the way to Portland. Joe was driving and he had Xerxes sitting up front with him. Emelina was still arguing when Joe and Xerxes put Julian and her on the shuttle to Seattle. Joe had said he would take care of the dog. Emelina was almost hoarse from her arguments by the time the shuttle landed at Sea-Tac airport and Julian commandeered a cab into town.

"I keep telling you this isn't the way Keith wants to handle it! The whole point is to try to keep his name out of this. That will be impossible if he goes to the cops!"

Julian smiled blandly. "You won't let me go to the police because you're afraid I'll be arrested, and you won't let your brother go because you're afraid his career will be ruined. Maybe we'll have to send *you* to the cops."

"Me!" That thought shut her up until the cab they were in reached the entrance to the highrise office building where her brother worked. By the time she was asking the receptionist to notify Keith of her presence her mind was churning with various alternative explanations she could give the police. They were certainly going to want to know how she had discovered what was going on at Eric Leighton's beach house! She fashioned one tale after another, plotting furiously.

"Emmy!" Five minutes later Keith Stratton stepped off the elevator into the lobby. Emelina looked at him with a touch of pride. Her brother was the perfect image of the fast-track corporate male. His dark chestnut hair, so much like her own, had been cut with a conservative razor and the chalk-striped suit he wore had been hand-fashioned by a tailor. Keith wore an aura of quiet authority with natural grace, and everyone he passed in the lobby nodded politely. Her brother was definitely in his milieu, Emelina decided with fond satisfaction.

"Emmy, what's going on? I thought you were down in Oregon." Keith gave his sister a quick kiss on the cheek and stepped back to slant a considering glance at the man by her side.

"I'm Julian Colter," said Julian, extending his hand. "And I would like to invite you to share a cup of coffee with Emmy and me down in the cafeteria. There are some things that need to be discussed."

If Keith wore the look of budding authority with natural instinct, Emelina decided, Julian wore the aura of well-established power with the confidence of a man who has wielded it for years. He had dressed for the trip to Seattle in a charcoal suit which fit his lean figure with a handcrafted look. The white shirt he wore also had a conservative, handmade appearance, and his subtly striped tie was of silk. Joe had brought the clothes along with him when he had been summoned from Portland. Dressed in her jeans and a button-down yellow preppy shirt, Emelina felt like an urchin next to these two masculine symbols of success.

It was funny, she thought as Keith nodded austerely at Julian and prepared to lead the way to the cafeteria, how success in the underworld looked a lot like success in the legitimate corporate field. If she hadn't known better, she would have guessed Julian to be a man at the top of the corporate ladder her brother was intent on climbing.

"So," Keith began conversationally as he got coffee for the three of them and found a booth, "how was your vacation, Emmy?" He shot his sister a shrewd glance.

"Julian knows all about my 'vacation,' Keith. You don't need to pretend around him," she sighed, sipping her coffee.

Keith said nothing, merely arching an inquiring brow at the older man. He wasn't going to commit himself until he learned just how much Julian knew, Emelina realized. Smart boy.

"Much to my everlasting astonishment," Julian drawled wryly, "your sister's crazy scheme worked. Your friend Leighton is using the beach house for less than legal purposes. He's running drugs down the coast. Once a month, to be exact. There will be another shipment the twenty-eighth of next month."

Keith stared from one to the other. "You're kidding!" His startled expression told Emelina all she had to know.

"I told you so!" she growled. "You didn't believe me when I told you he was up to something there, did you?"

"No," Keith retorted honestly. "I didn't." He turned to Julian. "That's why I let her go down there alone. But who the hell are you?" he demanded bluntly.

"Don't be rude, Keith. Julian helped me." Eagerly Emelina ran through the whole tale for her brother's sake. "It was Julian's idea to check the receipts in the grocery sacks. And he was with me on the beach the other night when Leighton and his crew arrived,'' she concluded. ''We've got all the proof you need, Keith.''

Keith absorbed the news, his eyes never leaving Julian's expressionless face. ''I see. But that still doesn't answer my question, does it? Who are you, Julian?''

For the first time since he had arrived in Seattle, Julian's mouth curved slightly. ''I'm the man who tried to save your sister from embarking on a career of breaking and entering and wound up doing the job myself. I was supposed to be taking a small vacation in the cottage down the street from the one your sister rented.''

''But who *are* you?'' Keith persisted doggedly.

''Never mind, Keith,'' Emelina interrupted firmly, unwilling to see Julian pinned down. Besides, she definitely did not want Keith to find out exactly who Julian really was. ''Julian has business interests along the West Coast,'' she explained. ''He lives in Arizona, though. He just had the misfortune of renting a cottage near mine, that's all.''

Keith gave her a level stare and then apparently decided to let the matter drop temporarily. Julian's smile edged upward as if he were secretly amused. ''Since my sister seems to have dragged you into this and you now know what's going on, what do you intend to do?''

''I was going to offer a little advice,'' Julian murmured.

''Such as?''

"How about giving what we know to the cops and finding out if they'd be interested in watching the Leighton house next month on the twenty-eighth? If they pick your blackmailer up in the middle of a dope transaction that should get him out of your hair. Leighton's unlikely to further incriminate himself by dragging your name into the picture. He'll have his hands full trying to get himself out of the smuggling charges."

"The police will ask a lot of questions, Julian," Emelina handled anxiously.

"I'll handle the police," he stated calmly.

"You will?" Keith watched him carefully.

"I will simply tip them off as to what I witnessed one night while vacationing on the Oregon coast. I'm sure the local cops will be happy enough to pursue it from there. Neither you nor Emelina will have to be involved."

Keith drew in his breath while Emelina stared. "That's very generous of you, Julian," he said quietly. "May I ask why you're choosing to be that generous?"

Julian's smile reached his eyes. "You're going to go far in the corporate world, Keith. You keep asking questions."

"Am I going to get some answers?"

Julian shrugged. "Isn't it obvious why I'm volunteering my help? I'm doing this for Emmy." He didn't look at her as he spoke, his whole attention on her brother. "She's become a close friend of mine."

"I see," Keith said quietly, ignoring the restless way his sister was moving in her seat. He assessed

Julian coolly for a long moment and then nodded. "I see," he said again. Emelina felt suddenly closed out of the conversation.

"If you two have finished with your man-to-man communication," she snapped irritably, "could we get on with some concrete planning?"

Keith smiled wryly. "Watch out for her when she starts in with that funny little habit of chewing on her lower lip," he advised Julian. "That's when she's at her most dangerous."

"I thought she did that when she was nervous or anxious," Julian said, turning to give Emelina a considering glance.

"No, she does it when she's scheming. Her imagination is very vivid," Keith warned.

"So I've learned."

Eight

It was the sight of Joe Cardellini's grimmer than usual expression as he greeted them in Portland that night that made Emelina realize wistfully how much she had hoped the idyll with Julian could have continued. She did not welcome the return to reality and neither, apparently, did Julian.

"What's up, Joe?" he demanded as he slid Emelina into the back of the Lincoln and followed.

"I had word from the Arizona office this afternoon, boss," Joe said quietly as he guided the big car out of the airport. "They've got some problems back in Tucson. Tony wants to talk to you ASAP."

Emelina withdrew into the corner of the seat, staring out the window as the two men conversed. She didn't want to know about this side of Julian's life, she realized.

"Tell Tony I'll call him first thing in the morning,

Joe. It'll wait that long at least?'' Julian's gaze was on Emelina's profile.

''Yeah. Not much you could do tonight, anyway, is there?''

''No. Drop us off at Emmy's apartment. No point going back to the beach until I find out what's happening down in Tucson.''

Emelina's head came around in mute question. Her apartment?

''Won't you give me a bed for the night, Emmy? Good friend of the family that I am?'' he asked softly.

She flushed, aware that Joe could overhear everything. Not that he didn't already know exactly what sort of relationship existed between his boss and herself, she thought.

''Does giving you a bed for the night constitute the first installment payment on my debt?'' she whispered with an attempt at flippancy.

''No,'' he shot back blandly. ''I'm asking for the room purely on the basis of our, er, friendship.''

She looked away from the gleam in his eyes and nodded. ''Yes, you can come home with me,'' she told him gruffly. What else could she say?

''Thank you, Emmy.''

Twenty minutes later she silently opened the door of her downtown apartment and switched on the hall light. Julian gazed at the surroundings with deep interest.

''Your vivid imagination extends to other things besides plotting and scheming, doesn't it?'' He grinned, examining the colorful, eclectic decor.

''I'm not too fond of pastels,'' she noted dryly,

following his eyes as he took in the bright yellow carpet, the green print furniture and the occasional touches of glossy black.

"No mauve?" he inquired blandly.

"I'm afraid not. Have a seat and I'll find us something to eat. I'm sure I left some stuff in the freezer." Emelina hurried into the crisp white kitchen and started opening cupboards and freezer doors. "How about some tuna fish on bagels?"

"Terrific." His voice sounded somewhat absent in tone, as if he were thinking of something else at the moment.

"Julian?" Curiously she went to the kitchen door and glanced into the living room. He was standing beside her typing table, looking down at a manuscript that she had left neatly stacked on one side. "Come away from there," she ordered huskily. "I've told you I don't let anyone read my work."

"Except faceless editors in New York?" he concluded, turning aside reluctantly. "Can't you make an exception for me, sweetheart? I already know so much about you and I want very badly to know even more."

"I'm sorry," she returned crisply. "I just don't make any exceptions to that particular rule."

"Not even for me, Emmy?" he coaxed gently, his eyes soft and searching.

"Not for anyone."

"Why not, honey?"

"It's too damn personal! That's why not. Now come in here and tell me how you like your tuna fish."

He sighed and came forward. "What are my options?"

"With onions or without," she told him stonily.

"Without."

Two hours later he tugged her into his arms on the couch and kissed her with lazy expectation. "That's why I chose to have my tuna fish without the onions," he told her when at last he freed her mouth.

"Oh," she said a little weakly. "You should have explained. Then I would have had mine without, too."

"It's all right, you taste delicious." He kissed her again, pulling her across his lap and cradling her close. "Emmy, I may have to leave in the morning," he whispered huskily, stroking the curve of her hip.

"Do you...do you think that whatever is going on down in Tucson will be that serious?" she asked, her brows drawing into a line of worry.

"Maybe. There were some things brewing before I left that may have erupted into a full-scale explosion."

"Oh, Julian," she breathed anxiously.

"Will you miss me if I have to go back in the morning?" he asked whimsically.

Emelina took a deep breath, aware of a deepening level of commitment. "Yes."

"Good," he retorted in satisfaction and leaned forward to find the line of her throat with his lips. A few minutes later when she began to twist restlessly under his hands Julian got to his feet with Emelina in his arms and headed for the bedroom.

There in the darkness Emelina surrendered with an

urgency tinged with fear of what awaited her on the morrow. She knew she could not keep Julian with her forever, but she had longed with all her heart for even a few more days together down on the Oregon beach. Something was already warning her that such an extension of the idyll was not to be.

It was the ringing of the bedside phone that awakened Emelina the next morning. She stirred lazily, reorienting herself, and then she recognized the compelling weight of Julian's arm across her breasts. She struggled to blink the sleep out of her eyes.

"Julian! The phone!"

"I hear it," he growled. "Ignore it. It's probably one of your *former* boyfriends."

"No one knows I'm here in town. Only Joe knows we're here." Emelina elevated herself on her elbow and reached for the receiver, knowing with deep foreboding who would be on the other end. "Hello?"

"Emmy? Joe. Is the boss there? I've got to speak to him right away."

Sadly she handed the phone over to Julian, who propped himself back against the pillows and let the sheet slide down to his waist. "Okay, Joe what's up?" he asked in resignation. "Okay, okay. I'll call him right now." He watched Emelina as she edged toward the side of the bed. Then he hung up and dialed another number. "Don't rush off, Emmy," he whispered as he waited for the phone to be answered on the other end. "You haven't kissed me good morning yet."

"You're like Xerxes," she groaned, trying to maintain a cheerful tone. "You think you have a right to affection from me whenever you want it!"

"You better believe it. Come and kiss me, sweetheart."

Her lips had just touched his when she heard the receiver click on the other end of the line. Reluctantly Julian freed her mouth and prepared to talk to the person in Tucson. Emelina hurried to the shower. She didn't want to hear the conversation that would take him away from her.

When Julian stepped into the shower stall behind her ten minutes later she knew the worst had come to pass. Without a word he wrapped his arms around her waist and leaned down to nuzzle her ear.

"You have to go to Arizona, don't you?" she whispered, aware of the hard warmth of him as he dragged her close to his naked length.

"I have to be back there this afternoon. Emmy, I wish I didn't have to go. Not so soon." There was a savage honesty in the words, and she took some comfort from them. Emelina could think of nothing more to say. Wordlessly she turned in his arms and pressed her soap-slick breasts against his chest, her hands going to his shoulders. She lifted her mouth to his and he took the offering hungrily.

"Joe will see about getting your car back from Oregon," Julian said quietly over breakfast. "I don't want you going near that place again, Emmy. Not until this is all over."

"You're so damn bossy," she complained, but she couldn't be mad at him. She was too afraid of the coming parting. They took a walk after breakfast while Joe confirmed Julian's flight reservations. Neither Emelina nor Julian mentioned the departure, itself, however. Neither wanted to talk about the inevitable.

It wasn't until it was time to leave for the airport that Julian lifted her chin with his forefinger and smiled gently down into her upturned face. "This isn't the end, honey. You know that, don't you?"

"I know." But next time it would be different between them. Next time she would be paying off the debt. "Oh, Julian, I wish..." She let the sentence trail off hopelessly.

"I'll phone you tomorrow night," he interrupted roughly and bent to brush his mouth against her own. "Be home."

"I'll see if I can work it into my schedule," she teased, but her hazel eyes were a little misty, and for some reason it was getting hard to swallow.

"You'd better," he rasped, not showing any sign of amusement over her attempt at lightness. "Or the next time I see you, I really will beat you."

"Promises, promises. I'll be here, Julian," she added quickly as his eyes narrowed. Clearly that was one subject he did not wish to banter about.

There wasn't any time to say more. Joe appeared in the open doorway and politely picked up Julian's bag. Emelina saw the hesitation on her lover's face and knew he wanted to say something else but couldn't quite find the words. The same was true for her. There were things that probably should have been said, but the relationship was still too new and there was still that debt hanging over her head.

On impulse Emelina stepped quickly over to the typing table and scooped up the manuscript lying there. "Here," she blurted, thrusting it into Julian's hand. "Take it. Something to read on the plane. Goodbye, Julian."

"Thank you, Emmy," he said quietly, glancing up from the manuscript to her face. He didn't say anything else. He kissed her a little roughly and then he was gone.

Emelina spent the next hour berating herself for having broken her own policy. What in the world had possessed her to give that manuscript to Julian?

By the time Emelina had finally grown philosophical about the matter, telling herself that there was nothing she could do to retrieve it now, Julian was settled into his seat on the jet to Tucson. The stewardess had just put a cup of coffee in his hand. Mindful of the ill effects of spilled coffee on white manuscript pages, Julian very carefully hauled out the precious package Emelina had given him. For a long moment he stared at the title page, aware of an absurd feeling of being on the verge of invading Emmy's privacy in an intensely personal manner.

Which was a totally ridiculous attitude, he told himself firmly. After all, she was hoping to get the thing published, wasn't she? It was meant to be read. And she had given it to him, herself. That last thought brought a wave of pure satisfaction, and Julian deliberately focused on the title of the manuscript: *Mindlink.* With rising eagerness he turned to the first chapter.

There he discovered a woman named Rana. She

was a heroine with an unusual problem. Born a non-telepath in a world where telepathy and the ability to link one's mind with another were the norm, Rana had been an outsider from the start. Not for her was the special kind of communication that existed when two humans linked minds. And not for her was the special relationship that came into existence when a man and a woman in love shared the intangible togetherness of mind-linking.

In an effort to escape the knowledge that she was a misfit, Rana had accepted a position as companion to the eldest daughter of a powerful house. She was to accompany the young woman off-world and conduct her to a neighboring planet in the system where the woman would be married to the head of an equally elite family. The job would give Rana a chance to get off her planet and perhaps free herself from the local star system entirely. Somewhere out there in the rest of the galaxy there were worlds where people like her, nontelepaths, were the norm. She had made up her mind to find one.

But first she had a job to do, and the responsibility of escorting the beautiful telepathic bride to her equally telepathic betrothed became very complicated when the ship on which they were traveling came under assault from enemies of the bride's husband-to-be.

Flung free in a crippled lifeboat while the main ship was under attack, Rana and her companion drifted helplessly in space, awaiting rescue. The problem, of course, lay in worrying over who would comprise the rescue party. The possibility that it would be the groom's enemies bent on kidnapping the bride was a strong one. By chapter two, Rana and her employer, Kari, were waiting, stranded, in the drifting lifeboat as the "rescue" party arrived and began forcing open the jammed airlock.

"It's useless, Rana," Kari wailed softly as she stared, stricken, at her companion. "Their minds are as closed to me as yours is! I can't even tell how many of them there are out there!"

"We still have the needle gun," Rana pointed out. "If we turn off the lights, we'll have a small advantage as they come through the airlock. They can only enter one at a time. The lock's too narrow to allow more than that." Her fingers clenched nervously around the tapered handle of the petite weapon she had found in the lifeboat's emergency stores.

"What good will that do us?" Kari shook her head. "Whoever it is out there will be armed to the teeth."

"It's the only chance we've got. Get behind the computer console, Kari. I'll need a clear line of fire." Great Helios! She'd never even fired a gun before in her life. Would she be able to pull the trigger of the one in her hand if it proved necessary? She flipped off the light.

There was no time for further thought. With a hiss, the inner door of the airlock slid open revealing a man's figure in a heavy spacesuit. The helmet was unlatched and thrown back, exposing the harsh planes of a rugged face.

"Kari of the House of Toran," he began with great formality, "I am Chal. I have been sent by the House of Lanal to rescue you. Do not be afraid."

"She's not afraid, just nervous around strangers," Rana forced herself to drawl coolly. She must sound as though she was in command of the situation. Men like this wouldn't bluff easily. "It's been an upsetting day. Enough to give a new bride a real case of jitters. Now suppose you convince us you're who you say you are."

The man who called himself Chal swung his suit light around in an arc until he picked out her figure crouched behind the console chair. He stilled as he saw the steady aim of the needle gun in her hand. "Who in Helios are you?" The formal tone of his voice had disappeared completely.

"The lady's traveling companion."

A slow, appreciative grin slashed across the man's face as he stood there regarding her. "Somehow I always thought of ladies' traveling companions as gentle, demure types."

"We've changed a bit over the years." Rana motioned with the needle gun. "Have one of your people set up a com link with the House of Lanal. I want to know who you really are before this goes any further."

"Yes, ma'am," he agreed mockingly, backing carefully toward the airlock. "Why don't you come and see me about employment when your present assignment is completed? I could use a traveling companion who takes her job seriously."

"Move!" Rana hissed, feeling a little desperate.

"I'm on my way. Just remember that when you're working for me I'll expect the same kind of service you're giving your present employer!"

Julian's mouth crooked gently as he read. There was something in Chal with which he could identify. And he wasn't at all surprised when the heroine wound up working for the space adventurer. There were thrills and excitement enough in Emmy's tale, but as he finished the last page Julian realized that what fascinated him the most was Emelina's handling of the fiery romance that developed between Rana and Chal.

Both were cursed with nontelepathic minds, minds that were forever closed to the magic of mind-linking. Living amid a society that depended on mind-linking as a means of assuring honesty and integrity, these two were forced to learn trust the old-fashioned way. For them, falling in love involved a risk that others never had to worry about. The telepaths around them knew exactly where they stood with one another, and when a telepathic man and woman fell in love there was never a question about the genuineness of their emotions. It could always be tested by mindlink. That certainty was denied Rana and Chal.

Yet through Emelina's imagination, a tender and deeply loving relationship grew between Rana and

Chal. A relationship that seemed somehow all the stronger and more enduring because it had to be built carefully.

So much of his sweet Emmy was in that manuscript, Julian realized as the plane touched down in Tucson. A sense of integrity, a lively imagination, a romantic outlook; all were caught between the pages of *Mindlink.* He walked to the baggage area to collect a disgruntled Xerxes, telling himself that he'd eventually have it all. He had to have it all. Like the hero in Emelina's novel, he had been living in a partially sealed off world until his woman arrived on the scene.

Emelina was still berating herself off and on over having given Julian a copy of the manuscript when the phone rang in Portland the next afternoon. She picked up the receiver to find the otherworldly voice of a New York editor saying she wanted to buy *Mindlink.*

As she set the phone back in its cradle with a shaking hand, Emelina no longer worried about the fact that Julian had read a copy of the manuscript. Instead she sat staring at the wall of her apartment with glazed eyes and wished with all her heart that Julian were there to help her celebrate. He was, she realized in a flash of blinding insight, the one man on the face of the earth with whom she wanted to celebrate the great event.

And she didn't even know his phone number in Tucson. There was, Directory Assistance informed her, no listing at all for Julian Colter.

By seven o'clock that evening Emelina had opened

the fifteen-dollar bottle of Cabernet Sauvignon she had purchased earlier in the day. The small dish of caviar was prepared and the stereo had been fed a tape of Mozart concertos.

Just as she was sitting down to enjoy all three in lonely splendor, the phone rang.

"Emmy?" Julian's voice was deep and soft on the other end of the line.

"Julian!" she breathed. "Oh, Julian, I sold the book! An editor called this afternoon! I tried to phone you, but I didn't have your number. My brother is in L.A. on an overnight business trip and there was no one to tell!"

"You sold *Mindlink?* Congratulations, sweetheart. But I can't say I'm terribly surprised," he chuckled. "I liked the book. Very much."

"You did?" Somehow that was as important as the editor's having liked it, she thought.

"Umm. It was full of you. How could I not enjoy it when I could find something of you on every page?" he said simply.

"Oh," she managed a little weakly.

"What are you doing?" he asked.

"Right now? Celebrating."

Instantly the pleasantness faded from his voice. "With whom?"

"Myself." She waited.

He sighed. "Do I sound possessive?"

Emelina decided to ignore that. "What are *you* doing?"

"Watching the evening news and petting Xerxes. He misses you, I think."

"Uh huh," Emelina muttered skeptically. "Sounds very homey."

"What did you imagine I normally do in the evenings?" he baited gently.

"I wouldn't dream of speculating."

"Sure you would. With your vivid imagination how could you help but speculate?"

"Julian, are you teasing me?"

"Only because I wish I was there helping you celebrate instead of here, patting my dog," he drawled wryly.

"Julian, I'm so excited," she whispered. "I think I'll quit my job tomorrow."

He laughed. "On the basis of one sale?"

"The editor said her publishing house is looking for a lot of books to fill a new line of women's adventure and science fiction. She feels my writing style will fit right in. They wanted another book as soon as possible."

"Hmm." He sounded abruptly serious. "Then we'd better see about getting you an agent, hadn't we? I don't think I want you taking on the New York publishing world all by yourself." Then he relaxed again. "Are you going to put your own personal adventures into a book?"

"That depends. Would you like to see yourself in a book, Julian?"

"Good God, no!" he retorted with great feeling.

"Then you'd better be very nice to me, hadn't you?" she taunted lightly.

"I see you're not averse to a little blackmail, yourself, honey. But as it happens, I have no objection to being very nice to you. If I were there right now, I would show you exactly what I mean."

"That sounds like another sexual innuendo," she accused.

"Sexual innuendoes are the most interesting kind."

"I get the feeling this conversation is about to degenerate into an obscene phone call!"

"It's okay. We're lovers," he assured her.

Long after he hung up that night Emelina considered the word. Lovers. As she stared with unseeing eyes at the remains of her caviar, she realized that, for her, at least, the word was a truthful one.

She was in love with Julian Colter.

Combined with the fact that she had sold her first manuscript, the realization was enough to make that particular day far too memorable.

In love with Julian Colter.

How had it happened? She knew instinctively that it wasn't because of what he could make her feel in bed. In fact, what happened to her when she was in his arms probably occurred precisely because she was in love, not the other way around.

She couldn't even begin to pinpoint the exact moment when she had taken that dangerous step over the edge of desire into love. But it had happened. She knew that now with absolute certainty.

She was in love with a man she knew almost nothing about and who held a very expensive debt over her head. Emelina surged restlessly to her feet and began clearing away the remains of her small celebration. What was he going to do? What happened to a woman who fell in love with a man like Julian Colter?

A man who wasn't even in the phone book, for heaven's sake!

What did he truly feel about her? There could be no doubting his desire, not after the way he had made love to her. And he could be trusted, she reminded herself. He had kept his end of the bargain they'd made.

Which only served to remind her that he would be expecting her to keep her end. She stiffened her shoulders as she carried the dishes to the sink. Julian would have no cause for complaint on that score. She always paid her debts. But how long would he go on wanting her after the situation with the debt was resolved?

Damn it, there were simply too many unknowns. All she could do was take it one day at a time. She headed back toward the telephone and made another attempt to contact her brother. Keith would want to know about the sale of the manuscript.

This time she got lucky. He was staying at the hotel he generally used while in Los Angeles, and his reaction was all she could have asked for.

"So you're going to quit your job, huh? Just like that?" he finally chuckled into the phone.

"I want to write full time, Keith. And the editor assured me that she would be very interested in the next book," Emelina told him excitedly.

"Well, I guess there's no harm in it. Even if the editor changes her mind, you won't starve to death, will you?"

"You mean you'll come to my rescue with a sack of groceries now and then?" she retorted.

"I don't think I'll have to worry about you, Emmy," Keith said easily. "You'll have Julian to make sure you get fed, won't you?"

"Julian!" she gasped.

"I had the distinct impression the man had staked a claim on you, sister. I don't see him relinquishing it very easily."

"But he's not... I mean we aren't...aren't planning on anything like marriage or—or even living together!" The protest came out in a fumbled manner as Emelina tried to get the message across to her brother. "Julian and I don't have what you'd call a...a relationship," she explained, unaware of the wistful note in her words. "We, uh, just got to know each other at the beach, and he offered to help with my scheme to trap Leighton. That's it, Keith, really it is."

"Sure it is." She could almost see him grinning into the phone. "Emmy, you don't have to play games with me. I'm your brother, remember? I know damn good and well you're in love with the man."

"Oh, Keith, what am I going to do?"

"Julian Colter can take care of his own," Keith said succinctly. "And he wants you. He'll look after you, Emmy."

"I don't particularly want to be looked *after*, you idiot!"

"I know," he sighed. "You want the promise of flaming love and eternal, torrid passion. But men don't have that sort of romantic outlook on life. You ought to know that by now. At least not men like Colter. Take my word for it, his type thinks in much more fundamental terms."

"You mean in terms of sex?" she asked icily.

"Yeah, that's one of them. Now tell me exactly what the editor said about your manuscript. When will the contract arrive? How much is she willing to pay up front? How about the royalty figures?"

"To tell you the truth I was too excited to ask all those questions," Emelina grumbled.

"Then I think we had better look into an agent."

"That's what Julian said," she groaned.

"I'm not surprised. The publishing business is definitely not one to enter with a pair of rose-colored glasses. I have a hunch it would chew a little romantic like you to pieces."

"You and Julian are very cynical!"

"We think alike on some things. I have a hunch Colter will take a very level-headed approach to the matter."

Like intimidating the publishers into paying the royalties on time? Emelina wondered with a wry grimace. Then she made a stab at changing the subject. "Keith, have you heard anything yet about Leighton?"

"No. After he gave me the ultimatum last month he said he'd be around to collect sometime next month. Julian called yesterday to suggest that I make the first payoff so Leighton wouldn't be suspicious. He's talked to the Oregon police, and they're going to watch the beach house on the twenty-eighth. If everything goes according to schedule, Eric should be out of my hair by the first of November. And that will be one hell of a relief,'' he added with a heartfelt sigh. ''What a mess. I don't know what we would have done without Colter. Things could have gotten awfully sticky.''

''Don't forget the whole thing was my idea!''

Keith laughed. ''And to think I thought it was all a harebrained scheme which would come to absolutely nothing. Goes to show a man should never underestimate his older sister, doesn't it?''

''I'm glad you've learned something from this mess,'' she said sweetly.

''Good night, Emmy. Remember what I said about getting an agent.'' Keith hung up the phone.

Could an agent deal with Julian Colter? she wondered with interest. Perhaps that was who she should send to negotiate the final payment of her debt. Determinedly she put the fanciful notion out of her head. She had no grounds for ''negotiating'' at all. She'd accepted Julian's help, making an unqualified promise to pay him in whatever way he demanded.

She always kept her promises.

The days slipped by as the twenty-eighth of the month approached. Keith called her one afternoon to inform her that he'd made the first payment to Eric Leighton. ''God, I'd like to see his face when the police pick him up with a suitcase full of dope next week!'' he'd concluded.

Julian phoned nearly every night, and she gathered from what little he said about the matter that he had his hands full in Tucson. She was afraid to ask too many questions. But he kept her informed of his dealings with the Oregon police and assured her that everything was on schedule.

"It'll be all over with next week, honey," he said as the twenty-eighth approached. "And this mess here in Tucson should be cleared up by then, too. That will leave us time for ourselves," he finished in satisfaction.

Emelina drew a deep breath and then said deliberately, "Julian, I want to get the debt out of the way. I don't want it hanging over my head."

"Don't worry," he told her coolly, "that's the first item on my agenda."

Emelina didn't know whether to be relieved or terrified as she hung up the phone that night.

Somehow the twenty-eighth finally arrived. Emelina was half tempted to return to the cottage she had rented on the beach just so she could observe the conclusion of the matter, but something told her that Julian would be absolutely furious if she went anywhere near the action. The thought of facing his fury just now was more than she could handle. She went back to her writing.

The phone rang on the morning of the twenty-ninth.

"It's all over, Emmy." Julian's voice sounded grim and remotely satisfied.

She shut her eyes briefly. "The police have Leighton?"

"Yes. I told your brother about it a few minutes ago. Leighton won't be bothering him anymore with blackmail attempts. He's going to have his hands full fighting the drug-running charges. And from what the police said, he doesn't stand a chance of getting out of them."

Emelina let out the breath she had been holding. "Thank you, Julian."

"Don't thank me," he muttered. "You're going to *pay* me, remember?"

"Yes." She sat very still, holding the phone as if it were made of heavy lead. Ever since the night when she had requested that the debt between them be cleared up as soon as possible, he had been almost cool on the phone. There had been no more teasing innuendoes or talk of being lovers. The phone calls since then had been far more businesslike and this one was the worst yet. There was no doubt that the warmth of their relationship was rapidly deteriorating, and Emelina didn't know how to salvage it.

"There are a few more things I have to clean up here in Tucson and then I'll be free to settle matters between us, Emmy," Julian went on in that cool, detached tone. "I'll call you the first of next week."

"Say hello to Xerxes for me," she instructed softly and gently replaced the receiver. She had to blink her lashes several times in order to clear away the moisture that had gathered behind her lids.

He was going to summon her next week to pay off the debt. What would he require of her?

Money? Perhaps. What an irony if she had replaced one blackmailer with another. She had no business contacts he would find useful. Her brother would have been the one to tap for that, and Julian had promised to keep her brother out of it. What did men like Julian Colter ask of people like her? Did power depend on having a bunch of little people in debt? Was that how the big crime syndicates worked? Or was it just instinctive for Julian to demand something in return for his assistance?

More than anything else in the world, Emelina wanted to pay off her debt to Julian Colter. Until she did, she would never know if there was really a chance for their relationship.

Nine

He had to do it before he lost his nerve completely.

What the hell was the matter with him, anyway? Everything was going according to plan. He knew Emelina would come when he called. Julian had never been more certain of anything in his life. All he had to do was pick up the phone and tell her to come to Tucson.

No, he corrected himself mentally, not *tell,* ask. There was no need to give Emelina an order. She would come to him, no questions asked, if he simply requested her presence. She owed him.

Request. That sounded unbearably arrogant, too.

Julian sat very still in the padded leather chair behind his ebony-colored desk and stared at his hands as he spread them out on the blotter. It almost looked for a moment as if his fingers were trembling. Grimly he closed the offending hands into frustrated fists.

Slowly he swiveled the leather chair around so that he could stare broodingly out the window of his fourteenth-floor office. It was a beautiful day in the desert city. In the distance the majestic mountains clawed a cloudless sky. The city basked under the seventy-five-degree warmth of a late fall day. Just the sort of day the tourists dreamed about.

But all Julian could think about was a foggy night at the beach. The urge to follow the mystery lady down the street as she slipped past his cottage had been irresistible. Even if Xerxes had not scratched at the door and whimpered expectantly, he would have stepped out into the chilled night and gone after her. In his mind Julian had been speculating for days about the nature of her interest in that deserted cottage.

He had watched her go into town in the mornings and return alone and had wondered if she were awaiting the arrival of a man, a lover. But no one had appeared. He had felt a sense of relief when no male showed up to claim the woman in the cottage down the street, a relief he hadn't wanted to fully acknowledge.

That night when he had followed her and found her trying to break into the old beach house, he had known he wouldn't be able to get the strange, restless curiosity out of his system until he had all the answers about the lady who lived down the street.

Yet the answers had only increased the restlessness and made him more thoroughly aware of her than ever. He could identify the physical desire easily enough. If what he felt had amounted only to that he could have handled it. He was a healthy, adult male, but he was not at the mercy of his physical needs.

Just as Emmy wasn't at the mercy of her newly discovered desire, Julian reminded himself. There had been more in their coming together than sex, and he knew it.

So why the hell was he terrified of picking up the phone and making the call that would bring her to Tucson? he challenged himself grimly. Why was he afraid to call in the tab? Emelina would pay. He could trust her.

There was no point putting off the day of reckoning. With an effort of will, Julian reached for the phone. If he waited any longer, he might lose his nerve completely. God knew it had been getting harder and harder to communicate with her long-distance. He'd been fully aware of her reaction to his increasingly stilted conversations. She had been gently withdrawing from him. There was no choice but to get her down to Tucson before the distance between them grew too great.

With great precision, Julian dialed Emelina's number. His hand was really shaking by the time he finally realized she wasn't home. Hell, he didn't dare put this off a moment longer. He cut the connection and dialed another number, that of Western Union. It might be easier to do this with a telegram, anyway, he assured himself. What a coward. It had been a long time since he'd been this scared. But, then, he consoled himself, perhaps a man was entitled to a few jangled nerves over a creature like Emmy Stratton.

When he'd finished dictating the message to the

Western Union operator, Julian called the Portland office and asked for Joe Cardellini. Joe came on the line immediately. No one kept Julian waiting.

"Yes, sir?"

Julian repressed a rueful smile as he heard the respectful tone in the younger man's voice. To think he'd once known a stab of jealousy when Joe had gently tried to soothe Emmy that morning in the cottage. Cardellini could be trusted, and even if he couldn't, Julian knew he could trust Emelina.

"Joe, I want you to make flight reservations for Emmy. She'll be coming down to Tucson on, let's see..." Julian broke off a moment, rubbing his temples as he tried to think. Better give her a couple of days to pack and make arrangements to be out of town. "On Thursday of this week. I'll have her call you to confirm."

"I'll arrange it," Joe said calmly.

"Yes, I know. Thank you, Joe. And thanks for the bugging work at the beach. Everything went perfectly on the twenty-eighth."

"Anytime, sir."

Julian replaced the receiver and continued to sit staring across the room, his fingers drumming uselessly on the desktop. It was done. In two days Emmy would be arriving at the airport. Carefully, largely to take his mind off his jitters, Julian began to make plans. He'd take her out to dinner at that plush restaurant in the hills overlooking the city. He'd make sure the chef knew ahead of time that Julian was arriving with a very special guest. That way they were certain to get the *escalopes de veau* and the best of the wine selection. Thoughtfully Julian decided he'd use the Mercedes with the top down so that when he drove her back to his house after dinner the wind and the stars would be in Emelina's hair. She'd like that. At home he'd have the cognac ready and some Mozart on the stereo. He recalled seeing Mozart in her tape collection. Desperately he racked his brain for anything he'd overlooked. Flowers. He'd have to see about getting some flowers. What else? Jewelry? Something simple in that line. Emelina wouldn't want flashy jewelry. Perhaps a little gold collar of a necklace. Yes, that would look good on her.

And then, when he'd paved the way with as many inducements as he could find, he'd tell her what he wanted in exchange for helping her brother.

Emmy would pay. She always paid her debts. And from now on, Julian decided, she would be in debt to no one but him.

The telegram was waiting for Emelina at six o'clock that night when she returned from the public library. She tore it open with shaking fingers and scanned the message inside.

I CAN'T WAIT ANY LONGER. COME TO TUCSON ON THURSDAY. CONTACT JOE FOR RESERVATION INFORMATION. I'LL BE WAITING AT AIRPORT. JULIAN.

Slowly she crumpled the flimsy paper. So Julian had summoned her at last.

In a way it was a relief. Emelina set down the groceries she'd picked up on the way home that evening and sank into the nearest chair, trying to collect herself. A *relief.* That's what it was. Didn't she want to get the whole thing over and done with? Of course she did. She would pay her debt and then see what remained of her relationship with Julian.

Two days. According to the telegram she had to wait two whole days. How could she possibly manage that? Her nerves would never survive the wait now that a deadline had been set! God! She had to get the whole thing over with as quickly as possible!

Impulsively she picked up the phone and dialed one of the airlines. There was no way in the world she could wait until Thursday. She would leave for Tucson tomorrow.

The ease with which she got reservations was frightening. Had she been subconsciously hoping that the airline would be booked? What was the matter with her? Emelina wondered as she hung up the phone and glanced down at her trembling fingers.

Nervously she got up and wandered into the kitchen to find something to eat. But when she had the cheese and sprout sandwich made she found it almost impossible to get down. Her stomach felt as if it had become a permanent residence for a flight of butterflies.

I'm turning into a nervous wreck, she realized grimly. It was ridiculous. Or was it? Her whole future hinged on what happened in the next twenty-four hours. The man she loved had summoned her to pay off a debt.

What would he demand of her?

All the tales she had ever read of how the Mob operated came back to her as she stood with the uneaten sandwich in her hand. It could be anything. Perhaps Julian wanted her to embezzle for him? No, that was ridiculous. She no longer even had an employer from whom she could steal! She'd quit her job two weeks ago.

Perhaps he needed an unknown woman he could infiltrate into some organization in Tucson. Would she be asked to serve as a Mafia spy?

The various possibilities whirled through her mind in vivid, living color, keeping her awake most of the night. Emelina spent the time packing and repacking the one suitcase she intended to take to Tucson.

In the end the one suitcase became three large cases. A woman never knew what she might need in a situation like this.

As soon as she thought Joe might be in the office the next morning, she phoned and asked for him. The phone was answered simply as "Colter & Co."

"Hello, Emmy. I've got your reservations all ready," he said easily as he came on the line. "I'm sure Xerxes will be looking forward to seeing you."

"Yes, uh, thank you, Joe. I was wondering if I could have Julian's home address just in case I miss him at the airport or something," she requested a little weakly.

"Huh? Oh, sure. Just a minute and I'll get it for you." Joe came back on the line shortly and read her off the address. "But I wouldn't worry about missing him. I get the feeling he'll be waiting at the airport with bells on his toes."

"An interesting image," Emelina smiled wryly.

"Yes, it is, isn't it?" She could sense Joe's slow smile. "Well, you can pick up your tickets at the airline counter on Thursday. Or would you rather I came by and took you to the airport?" he added quickly.

"Oh, no, that won't be necessary," Emelina said hurriedly, wishing she didn't have to deceive Joe. "A friend is going to take me."

"Okay. Call if you need anything else."

"Thank you, Joe," she murmured humbly.

"Anything for Julian's lady," he told her emphatically.

Emelina hung up the phone, turning the words over in her head. Julian's lady. No, she couldn't really be Julian Colter's woman until after they had cleared up the business between them. And by then the chasm between them might be far too wide to cross.

What if Julian asked something absolutely impossible of her? What would she do then? Emelina shuddered as she thought of such assignments as putting poison in a competitor's tea.

No, Julian wouldn't operate in that fashion, she assured herself in the next breath. She had the feeling from the way he communicated with Keith that he handled his business in a very modern corporate style. Julian was no back-alley thug or former killer. And everyone knew the modern Syndicate was into all sorts of legitimate businesses.

Yes, Julian would be in something that was reasonably legitimate, Emelina told herself as she hauled her three suitcases down to the basement garage. It might not do to inquire too carefully into his background, but surely his current operations would be relatively businesslike.

In which case the question of what he could want from her became even more confusing.

The flight to Tucson was uneventful, but Emelina arrived with nerves that felt as if they had just ridden out a thunderstorm. She managed to get herself and the three huge suitcases into a cab and from there into a modern motel, but shortly thereafter she felt as if she were going to collapse.

Action, that was what she needed. She would case the situation and make plans. Hastily she threw on a pair of jeans and button-down shirt and hurried out of the motel to find another cab.

"Could you please drive me past this address?" she requested, climbing into the backseat.

"Sure," the driver said equably. "You don't want to stop?"

"No, I just want to cruise past." She sat back in the seat and watched eagerly as the driver took her out to an expensive area of town. The houses were set wide apart on lots that were landscaped to blend in with the desert surroundings. They slowed as they went by a modern house done in stark white and built around an interior courtyard. Wrought-iron gates protected the inviting garden inside. There was no way of telling if anyone was at home.

"This is it, ma'am," the driver said. "You want to go by again?"

"No. Once is enough," she whispered, staring out the back window at the beautiful, expensive home. "Thanks."

"You bet." The driver shrugged. It wasn't his business.

So much for casing the joint, Emelina decided back in her motel room as she paced the floor. Now what? It was getting close to five o'clock. Perhaps a little food would settle her stomach before she called another cab.

What was she going to wear for the big reunion? After unpacking all three suitcases, Emelina decided that nothing she had brought along seemed appropriate for the occasion ahead of her. She wound up showering and putting on her jeans again.

Standing in front of the mirror she piled her hair into a loose knot on top of her head. The Oxford cloth shirt and jeans appeared very functional, she told herself. Then she headed downstairs toward the restaurant next to the motel.

Nothing on the menu, however, looked as though it would settle her stomach.

"I'll have a margarita," she finally announced to the hovering waitress. Perhaps a little alcohol would unjangle her nerves. Emelina glanced at her watch. It was going on six o'clock. What time did Julian get home from work?

Twenty minutes later she was so pleased with the effects of the first margarita she ordered another. The salt on the rim tasted especially good.

Twenty minutes after that she glanced at her watch again and told herself Julian might have been delayed in getting home from the office. No sense rushing out to his house.

"Another margarita?" the waitress inquired as she drifted past Emelina's table.

It was all the encouragement Emelina needed. "Yes, please."

"Perhaps some chips?" the woman suggested gently, surveying the rather strange gleam in her customer's eyes.

"That sounds lovely," Emelina decided, feeling much more cheerful.

When the chips arrived she downed them along with the third margarita. The drinks were working, she decided in satisfaction. Her stomach felt almost normal. It was too bad her head was beginning to feel slightly detached from her body. But it seemed to make it easier to think clearly.

"That was a lovely dinner," she confided to the waitress as the woman came by a fourth time. "But I think I'd better be on my way. No sense putting this off any longer, is there?"

"Probably not," the waitress agreed, stifling a smile as Emelina very carefully extricated herself from behind the small table. "Are you driving, ma'am?" she added with a genuine touch of concern.

"Heavens no! I was going to call a cab. I don't know my way around Tucson, you see."

"I'll, uh, call it for you, ma'am," the woman volunteered.

"That's very kind of you." Emelina tipped lavishly and walked with great precision toward the door.

When the cab arrived she settled herself thankfully

into the seat. It had been difficult standing up, she'd discovered. "I want to go to this address, please."

"Sure," the young man said, hiding a smile as he studied his inebriated fare. He made sure her door was closed securely and then headed for the exclusive suburb. "Looks like you got an early start on the party," he murmured as he pulled the cab to a halt in front of the modern home a short while later.

"Party? What party?" Emelina opened her eyes. They had been closed most of the way from the restaurant. She blinked owlishly.

"There seems to be a party here tonight," the driver explained as he glanced into his rearview mirror. "The cars are parked clear up to the next intersection."

"Oh, I see." Emelina decided the man was right. Julian's drive was filled with vehicles which poured out into the street and lined the block. "Well, that's just too bad. I'm going inside anyway! How much do I owe you?"

He told her the sum and Emelina added a five dollar bill to cover the tip. "I'm feeling quite generous tonight," she explained gravely as he started to protest.

"Well, thank you," the driver said uncertainly and then jumped out to help her open the door. She was having some trouble with it.

"Good night and thank you," Emelina said politely. With her chin high in a regal gesture, she started up the walk to the open wrought-iron gate. Somewhere in that house was Julian, and she wasn't going to turn around and leave now, even if he was giving a party. Deep in the foggy recesses of her brain Emelina knew that she would have great difficulty working up her present level of courage again tomorrow night.

No one stopped her as she walked through the gate into the beautifully landscaped courtyard. Soft lanterns lit the handsomely dressed men and women who filled the garden. The laughter and chatter carried easily into the night, and Emelina decided that it sounded genuine. Good. If everyone here was enjoying himself or herself, then Julian probably was, too. He would be in an excellent mood, she decided craftily. It would be an ideal time to hit him up about that stupid debt.

A few people turned to glance enquiringly at her as she came through the gate. When they realized they didn't recognize her they smiled and turned back to their conversations. A few cast interested glances at her jeans, but no one stared rudely.

Off to one side, near an open glass door, Emelina spotted the bar that had been set up to serve the guests. Instinctively now she headed for it.

"A margarita, please," she requested gently of the politely inquiring bartender. "I'm going to mingle."

"This will no doubt help," he agreed, fixing the drink. "Here you go."

"Thank you. Have you seen Julian?" Emelina licked the salt off the rim of her glass and leaned back against the bar. The support was welcome. She scanned the cheerful throng.

"He came by a few minutes ago," the bartender said. "I think he was headed in that direction." He nodded vaguely toward the opposite corner of the garden.

Emelina braced herself with one elbow and followed the bartender's glance. There, in close conversation with two other men, stood Julian. He was sipping casually at a glass which appeared to contain scotch on the rocks and looking very much at ease in a conservatively cut evening jacket and slacks of near black. In the lantern light his dark hair gleamed, and harsh shadows fell on the rugged planes of his unhandsome face. He was deeply intent as he talked to the two men who stood with him.

"Isn't he beautiful?" Emelina whispered to the bartender.

The bartender arched one brow. "Well, to tell you the truth, I hadn't thought of him in quite that way," he hedged carefully, unwilling to engage in open argument with one of Colter's guests.

"He is, you know," Emelina confided helpfully. "Oh, I'll admit he's no movie star, but I was never the type to fall for movie stars, anyway. There's something else about Julian."

"Women are often attracted to power," the bartender observed with surprising insight.

Emelina shook her head emphatically. "No, that's not it. Many of my brother's friends have power and I've never fallen for them. No, the thing about Julian is that you can trust him, you see. He always upholds his end of a bargain." She took another sip of the margarita.

"You've got a point there," the bartender conceded thoughtfully. "He's got a reputation in this town. Always does what he sets out to do, or so I hear. Pays his hired bartenders well, too,'' he added with a grin.

''These people,'' she gestured at the assembled crowd. ''They're all friends of his?''

''Friends and business acquaintances. Colter gives two parties like this a year to repay his social obligations. I don't think he particularly enjoys them, though.''

''No,'' Emelina smiled sunnily. ''He's really a quiet type at heart, isn't he?''

''Well, I wouldn't know too much about that,'' the man said hastily. ''Nobody talks about him being a playboy, though. Keeps his love life quiet and out of the public eye. You a close friend of his?''

''I owe him,'' Emelina explained very seriously. ''I'm here to pay off a debt.''

''I see.'' The bartender sounded vaguely mystified and appeared to be on the verge of risking another question when a fierce, joyous barking shattered the civilized hum of conversation. ''Oh, hell, that damn dog got loose! Colter will be furious. It was supposed to be locked up in the backyard!''

As if on cue the entire crowd turned to stare at the open gate as Xerxes came tearing around the corner and burst upon the scene. The sleek Doberman announced his presence with another loud *whoof* and then he bounded straight for Emelina.

''Xerxes!'' Julian's voice rapped sharply in the sudden silence. ''What the hell!... *Emelina!*''

Julian stared at the figure going down beneath the happy assault of the Doberman. Xerxes had managed to knock her completely off balance and was standing over her as she lay flat on her back on the grass. For an instant Julian felt absolutely frozen in astonishment and then he managed to unglue himself from where he was standing and stride quickly across the garden to the pair on the lawn.

"Nice dog, nice dog," Emelina was saying breathlessly, pushing ineffectually at the happy dog. "Down boy. Let me up, Xerxes. I have to get up."

"Xerxes! Sit!" This time Julian's voice brooked no argument, and the dog responded obediently, sitting on his hind haunches beside Emelina.

"Oh, Julian," Emelina muttered trying to sit up and brush herself off. "There you are. Thank you for calling off your dog. I suppose he means well," she allowed grudgingly, "but he's so *aggressive!*"

Julian stared at the rumpled figure sitting on the ground beside his dog. Emelina's hair had come free of the clip that was supposed to be holding it back and cascaded in disarray around her shoulders. The jeans she wore were faded and had shrunk until they hugged her full hips. The maize-colored shirt was stained from the grass and as he took in the oddly bright expression in her hazel eyes Julian realized that his sweet Emmy was more than a little tipsy. The margarita she had been holding in one hand when Xerxes appeared had splashed on her jeans.

Julian realized that he was torn between a wave of affectionate amusement and sudden fear. She was here. Not precisely in the right place at the right time or in the right condition, but she was here. He reached down to lift her to her feet.

"Emmy, you sweet idiot. What the hell do you think you're doing?"

"Paying off my debt," she explained politely as she stood in the circle of his arms and stared up at him with a serious mien.

"Of course," he drawled very dryly. "What else would you be doing. Come inside, Emmy. George," he added brusquely, signaling to the bartender. "Take Xerxes back to the other yard and see he's properly chained this time."

"Right away, Mr. Colter," the man said obediently, reaching rather tentatively for Xerxes's collar. "Come on, dog."

Xerxes didn't move, his dark eyes on Emelina. The bartender tugged carefully. The dog ignored him.

"Let him come with us, Julian," Emelina sighed. "He's such a stubborn sort of dog. Rather like you."

Julian groaned, feeling as if the situation had exploded in his hands. He'd never felt so out of control in his life. "Forget it, George. Come on, Xerxes," he growled and turned to walk through the open door, his arm still around Emelina. The dog followed at a brisk pace, and the crowd settled back into amused conversation.

"Trust you not to follow the plan," Julian sighed as he eased Emelina into a large chair and went to the sideboard to pour himself another scotch. He needed it, he realized grimly.

"Could I have another margarita?" Emelina inquired blandly, watching him as he paced once across the room and back in front of her. It was a charming room, done in the Spanish style with heavy beams and whitewashed walls. The furniture was equally heavy and much of it looked hand carved.

"Sorry, I don't have the makings for a margarita here," he told her roughly and instantly regretted his tone of voice. What was the matter with him? He didn't want to get her upset by yelling at her! Why the devil did she have to arrive drunk? On the other hand, maybe that would make things easier. "Would you like a glass of wine?" he offered apologetically.

"That would be lovely." She smiled at him serenely.

"Emmy, you are bombed out of your charming little skull, aren't you?" he groaned as he poured the wine.

"I had a lovely meal at the restaurant next to my motel," she explained placidly.

"I'll bet. How many margaritas?" He handed her the wine and frowned. She had to use both hands to hold the glass upright.

"I don't remember. But there were chips. The waitress brought me some chips."

He listened to the overly careful emphasis on each word and shook his head ruefully. Then he took a sip of his own drink and lowered himself into the chair across from her. Xerxes sprawled between them, a happy dog. "I can't figure out whether your being drunk is going to make this easier or harder," Julian confessed, stretching out his feet and leaning back into his chair. He watched her from under narrowed lids.

"Oh, it makes it much easier," she told him cheerily, downing a swallow of wine. "It needs salt," she informed him, examining her glass.

"Which needs salt? The wine or our conversation?" he grumbled. Damn, he could feel his fingers trembling again. He clutched them more tightly around the glass.

"The wine. As far as our conversation goes, I'm not sure what it needs." Emelina frowned and shook her head. "No, that's not true. It needs to get over and done, I think."

"You're right," he agreed, trying to take a grip on himself. "But first tell me why you jumped the gun. Why are you here tonight instead of on Thursday?"

"I couldn't wait. I was getting very nervous, Julian." She regarded him with wide eyes. "I hate being in debt."

"Emmy, honey," he began softly, wanting more than anything else in the world to take that reproachful look out of her eyes. "Will it be so very difficult?"

"Paying the debt?" She blinked sleepily. "That rather depends on what you ask of me, doesn't it?"

"I suppose." And in spite of his determination, Julian found he still couldn't quite bring himself to tell her what it was he would be requiring of her. What if she turned him down? No, he reminded himself in the next second, she wouldn't refuse. She'd pay. His knuckles whitened around the cold glass in his hand. Of course she would pay. *Tell her what you want, you fool.* "Does Joe know you're here?" In disgust he heard himself ask the unimportant question instead of the important one.

"Nope." Emelina shook her head emphatically. "He thinks I'm going to be on the three-ten flight tomorrow. I tricked him," she declared proudly.

"So I see. I'll have to have a word with him," Julian said dryly. Instantly Emelina looked stricken.

"No! You mustn't be upset with him! It's not his fault. It's mine!"

"That doesn't surprise me."

"Julian," she began very firmly. "You're not to get angry at Joe. Promise me you won't be mad at him. He did as he was told!"

"Okay, I won't be mad at him," Julian capitulated, realizing that there was really no point in trying to conduct any kind of argument with Emelina tonight. And he didn't want to risk annoying her now. The discussion about Joe was only one more delaying tactic.

Another such tactic mercifully appeared from the direction of the garden as George the bartender traipsed embarrassedly through the room. "Sorry, boss. We're out of ice. I'll just be a minute."

There was dead silence in the living room as the young man hurried on through into the kitchen and then reappeared with several sacks of ice. He nodded quickly at Emelina, who smiled benignly back at him and then disappeared again into the garden.

"A very nice man," Emelina remarked to Julian. "I've met a lot of nice people today. Cab drivers, waitresses, bartenders. Everyone's been most kind." She raised her glass in a salute. "Here's to kind people everywhere."

Julian's mouth turned down wryly as he watched her drain the last of the wine. "Do you number me among the folks who have been kind to you, Emmy?" he asked softly.

"Oh, definitely," she assured him. "Could I have another glass of wine?"

"Honey, I think you've had enough."

She shook her head. "No, not enough. I can still think a little. Be kind to me, Julian, and fetch me another glass of wine. There's a good boy."

He rose reluctantly and took the wineglass. "You don't have to talk to me as if I'm Xerxes."

"You two are a lot alike," she countered firmly.

"Maybe we're both just hungry for affection?" he suggested as he handed her back the half-filled wineglass. Damn it! He was going to have to get this over with as soon as possible. His pulse was thudding heavily and the palms of his hands were damp. Julian felt like an idiot. Abruptly, he also felt a little incensed. Nothing was going according to plan! "Hell, Emmy, this wasn't the way I wanted to do it! I was going to take you out for a beautiful dinner and drive you through the desert night with the top down on the car and then bring you back here and serve you cognac..."

"And seduce me?" she concluded brightly.

"No! At least not right off," he amended in a flash of honesty. He lounged back in his chair and tried to muster his courage. "No, Emmy, I wasn't going to seduce you until after you had agreed to pay the debt," he ground out.

"Ah! Now we come to the heart of the matter.

What, exactly, are you going to require of me, Julian? I warn you, I'm not very good at spying or embezzling or various forms of mayhem. Also, I feel I should warn you that I no longer have a regular income. You will have to wait right along with me for the royalties to arrive if it's money you want.'' She faced him boldly, chewing on her lower lip.

Julian stared back at her, every fiber of his body taut and aware. ''Emmy,'' he said gently. ''I don't want your money. I don't want you to spy for me or embezzle for me. I want something only you can give me. I want you to come and live with me here in Tucson.''

Emelina frowned at him. ''Say that again?''

''You heard me,'' he growled, suddenly terrified. ''Give me your word that you'll come and live with me, Emmy. I need you.''

''*That's* what you want in payment of the debt?'' she gasped.

''Yes.'' The single word came tightly through his teeth.

She stared at him a second longer and then slowly, emphatically shook her head. ''No.''

Julian felt the blood drain from his face as he absorbed the impact of the single word. It was like absorbing the impact of a body blow. A wave of helpless anguish washed over him. *He loved her!* He hadn't fully realized it; hadn't wanted to acknowledge the depth of his own emotion. He loved her and she was rejecting him. Julian felt as if the world around him had just crumbled.

There was a frozen silence in the living room as

Emelina and Julian faced each other. Xerxes lifted his head questioningly, sensing the strained atmosphere and uncertain what to do about it.

From somewhere Julian managed to find the energy to speak. The effort seemed to take everything he had. "I thought," he rasped dully, "that you always paid your debts."

Emelina yawned and patted her mouth politely. "Oh, I do, Julian. But I would never come and live with you in order to uphold a *bargain.*"

"I see." My God! What was he going to do now? Julian wanted to rage or accuse or condemn. She had promised him that she would pay her debt! She had given him her solemn word! And now she was reneging on it. Never had he felt so incredibly helpless or so incredibly desperate.

Emelina yawned again and set down her wineglass. She leaned comfortably back into the corner of the chair and curled her legs under her. Her lashes settled on her cheeks. "I will come and live with you, Julian," she murmured sleepily, "not because of the bargain, but because I love you. It's not fair to tease me, though. In the morning you must tell me what it is you really want in exchange for our deal at the beach."

Julian surged to his feet, nearly tripping over Xerxes as he took one long stride toward Emelina's chair.

But there was nothing more to be said that night. Emelina had passed out very comfortably in the padded leather chair.

Ten

Emelina opened her eyes the following morning to find an apparition sitting at the foot of the bed holding a cup of coffee.

"Good lord, Julian," she groaned, her hand going to her aching head, "you look worse than I feel." She surveyed his burning dark eyes, the rumpled pelt of his hair and his obviously slept-in shirt and slacks. "Must have been some party."

"It was," he rasped dryly. "Actually, it was a little dull until you arrived, but between you and Xerxes things managed to liven up considerably."

Xerxes, who was standing guard at the side of the bed, shoved his nose at Emelina's outflung hand and she automatically patted him. "Stupid dog," Emelina murmured affectionately. "Oh, God, my head hurts."

Julian moved forward with the coffee and held it out to her. "Here. This will help."

"I doubt it." But she struggled to a sitting position against the pillows and took the cup with unsteady hands. Julian's eyes never left her face. "I guess I look pretty bad, don't I?" she sighed.

"You look beautiful." He half smiled.

There was a tentative silence while Emelina sipped her coffee and considered the precarious state of her stomach. Then, in an effort to break the lengthening lull in the conversation she said very politely, "You have a lovely home, Julian."

He ignored that, his gaze still intent on her strained features. "Emmy," he whispered, "how much do you remember about last night?"

She frowned, trying to recall the details. "Why?" she demanded suspiciously. "Did you take advantage of me?"

"Of course not!" he denied gruffly.

"Too bad. Well, as long as I didn't miss anything, I guess I can't complain."

"Emmy, stop teasing me or I'll..." He broke off helplessly.

"Or you'll what? Beat me?" She smiled blandly. "There's no need to turn violent, Julian. I already feel as if I've been through a war."

"Damn it, Emmy, did you mean what you said last night?" he grated, his hands tightening in frustration.

"Could you be more specific?"

"About loving me!" he almost snarled and then he had the grace to look ashamed. Julian sucked in his breath, clearly striving for patience. "Emmy, did you mean it when you said you'd come and live with me not because you owed me but because you loved me?''

''Oh, that,'' she murmured with a breeziness she wasn't exactly feeling. ''Of course I meant it.'' How blind a man could he be about a woman, she thought wonderingly. ''Didn't you know I loved you?'' she whispered gently.

He looked at her with raw hunger. ''No.'' He shook his head dazedly. ''That is, I didn't think of it in those terms. I only thought about tying you to me, making you mine. Seeing to it there were no escape clauses. I never thought about love.''

''Probably because you don't believe in it,'' she retorted tartly. ''But that's the only thing that would tie me down, Julian. Did you really think you could have me in exchange for doing me a favor?''

''You said you always paid your debts,'' he ground out carefully.

''Love isn't something one can bargain for. Even if I wanted to pay you that way, I couldn't have faked it. You forbade me to fake that sort of thing, remember?'' she taunted softly.

''That was sex, Emmy. That had nothing to do with love.''

''Didn't it?'' she whispered. ''Perhaps not for you, Julian, but it did for me. Somehow it all comes bound up in a single package when I'm with you. The love and the sex and you and your dog.''

Reluctant amusement edged his hard mouth as Xerxes inched closer to Emelina. ''You're determined to make a joke out of this, aren't you?''

She winced. ''Surprisingly, I don't feel in much of

a joking mood this morning. Did I make a terrible fool of myself last night?''

Julian put out a hand and pushed some of the straggling chestnut hair off her face. His eyes softened with infinite tenderness as he smiled down at her. ''No, sweetheart. I'm the one who made a fool of myself. I didn't realize I'd fallen desperately in love until the moment you told me you wouldn't come and live with me. I felt as if my whole future had just been shattered like a mirror. Until that point I kept telling myself that if I could get you to agree to come to me as part of our deal, I would be guaranteeing myself a woman who was faithful, loyal and completely trustworthy.''

''Sort of like a nice dog, hmmm?'' But Emelina's mouth gentled as she waited for him to go on. A strange warmth moved through her as he confessed his love.

He grimaced. ''I'll admit I've grown rather cynical about relationships based on attraction. That's about all my first marriage had going for it. I decided a relationship based on integrity might have a better chance.''

''I think you're right as far as it goes. You just didn't think it all the way through,'' Emelina decided, trying another sip of coffee. ''Real love seems to demand some risk taking, doesn't it?''

''Emmy, when did you realize you loved me? When did you decide to take the risk?'' he asked tightly, thinking of the risk her characters in *Mindlink* had taken.

''I'm not sure,'' she replied honestly. ''I kept feeling more and more *committed.*'' Emelina broke off, her brows drawing together accusingly. ''Which was exactly what you wanted me to feel, wasn't it?''

Julian nodded slowly. ''I wanted you to feel so bound to me you wouldn't be able to break free. No, don't say it. I already know I'm selfish, arrogant and ruthless.''

''Well, you can't be all bad. Xerxes likes you.''

''Emmy! Here I am trying to make a confession of love and you keep bringing my dog into the picture!''

''Didn't you once say, 'Love me, love my dog'?'' she inquired.

''And you once said something about having to take your coffee along with you,'' he reminded her indulgently.

''Has it come to that? You're even willing to tolerate my coffee?'' she breathed, her eyes shining in spite of the terrible way she felt.

''I think I can figure out something to do about the coffee. I *know* I can figure out something to do about it. As long as I know I can have you,'' he added bluntly. ''Emmy, I love you. I think I must have loved you from the first. I've never wanted a woman the way I want you. I've never plotted and planned and coerced to get a woman before.'' He looked stricken by the lengths to which he had gone.

''I was so afraid at times during the past few weeks that you were withdrawing from me,'' she confessed, remembering the increasingly stilted phone conversations. ''When you left Portland I thought we had some kind of understanding, at least. I thought there was hope for a relationship. But you kept getting more and more distant on the phone.''

"Because I kept getting more and more terrified of what would happen when I finally demanded that you come to Tucson and live with me,'' he muttered. "On the one hand I kept telling myself you would do as I asked because you always paid your debts. But I was scared, Emmy. Scared in a way I've never been scared before in my life. I suppose I knew, deep down, that a man can't bargain for the kind of thing I wanted from you. I knew it amounted to so much more than physical attraction, but I was afraid to put a name to it until last night. Oh, Emmy, you ruined everything by arriving a day early, do you realize that?'' he groaned. "I had everything planned.''

"My nerves would never have survived another day,'' she pointed out.

His mouth crooked wryly. "Mine might not have either. Last night was hard enough on them!''

"What did happen last night?''

"After you passed out on me with that immortal exit line about loving me? I carried you off to bed and put Xerxes on guard. Then I spent the rest of the evening running back and forth between my guests and you. I was determined to be around when you finally woke up, you see. I wanted to make sure I'd heard correctly!''

"Didn't you go to bed?'' She scanned his disheveled figure.

"I went to bed.'' He indicated the other side of the wide bed on which she lay. "I slept, sort of, over there. Mostly I just looked at the ceiling and wondered how long you were going to sleep. It was probably the longest night of my life, Emmy. I don't ever want to go through another one like it. Will you marry me, sweetheart?''

Emelina's reeling stomach stilled for just a moment. ''The last offer I heard was to come and live with you.''

''For the rest of our lives,'' he clarified a little huskily. ''Which means you might as well marry me. Please, Emmy!''

Instead of answering, she merely searched his haggard face. ''You're not really a gangster, are you?''

''You sound disappointed,'' he retorted wryly.

''Well, marrying a genuine Mafia chieftain would have given me some great research material for my next book,'' she pointed out thoughtfully.

''Emmy! For God's sake! Put me out of my misery!'' he thundered.

''Yes, Julian. I'll marry you.'' She used her meekest tones.

He reached for the coffee cup in her hand, removed it and set it on the bedside table. Then he made to gather her close. ''When,'' he growled, his face less than five inches away, ''did you decide I might be a legitimate businessman?''

''When I started realizing that you and my brother shared a few traits in common. And then last night when I saw all those nice people who were your friends, I began to realize you were probably just an ordinary businessman.''

''A rather dull sort for a writer to marry?'' he queried grimly.

Emelina managed a smile. "Not at all. I have the feeling you will be a source of great inspiration, in fact. Julian, I love you so. And, frankly, although it might have been terribly exciting to be a Syndicate wife, I'm rather relieved that we'll be able to live a normal life."

"Honey, I don't see any life with you ever ranking as 'normal'!" he told her feelingly.

"Why did you let me and everyone else go on thinking you were an underworld figure hiding out?" she demanded.

He shrugged. "I didn't care what the townspeople thought. They probably got the idea from watching me arrive in the company limousine. And they saw Joe a couple of times. I guess that probably added to the impression."

"An impression you were too arrogant to correct!"

"Maybe," he agreed noncomittally. "I was there on the beach for a much needed rest. I kept to myself and I didn't want to be bothered."

"Uh, what exactly *is* your business, Julian?" Emelina asked cautiously.

"I run a chain of hotels in the Western states."

"And good old Joe really does look after 'security'?"

"Yes. Hotel security is very sophisticated stuff. Joe has quite a background in it. Not that he goes around bugging guest rooms," Julian hastened to add quickly.

"I should hope not!"

"Emmy, honey, I'm sorry I didn't tell you the whole truth, or at least straighten out your misconceptions about me,'' he said seriously. ''But I wanted to give you the impression I really could help your brother and I suppose I thought you might believe I was capable of handling a man like Leighton if I had some underworld connections.''

''You know what I think?'' she retorted. ''I think you let me go on believing you were a hood because in your arrogance you liked the notion of my falling for you even though I thought the worst!''

He looked pained. ''Sweetheart! How could you imagine something that ruthless? Never mind,'' he added immediately. ''I just answered my own question. You are capable of imagining a great deal! Which should give you a long and interesting career as a writer.''

Julian leaned closer, his mouth hovering above hers, his intentions plain. ''God, I love you, honey. I can't even imagine living without you now that I've found you.''

''Julian,'' she asked deliberately, ''I don't think now is a good time to kiss me.''

He stilled. ''Why the hell not?''

''Because I think I'm going to throw up.''

Three days later Emelina smiled down at the plain gold band on her left hand and studied it with pleasure as she sprawled languidly on the wide lounger in Julian's garden. ''Do you know, darling,'' she drawled thoughtfully as her husband came through the sliding glass door with two glasses and a bottle of champagne in his hand, ''I'm beginning to have some suspicions about why you married me.''

He groaned, setting down the glasses and pouring champagne into each. "Let's hear what that over-reactive imagination of yours has come up with this time!"

"Well, it occurred to me during the ceremony this morning that there are a lot of vows and promises made during the marriage service."

"Isn't that the truth, though?" Julian sounded as if the notion had only just occurred to him, too. He handed her a glass and sank down into the padded lounger beside her. Xerxes walked around in circles at the foot of the wide chair and then settled down peacefully.

"Did you decide to marry me because you realized that I'd be sure to honor my wedding vows?" Emelina nestled in the curve of her husband's arm, not particularly alarmed at the possibility of Julian's having ulterior motives.

"Nope, that was merely a fringe benefit," he assured her equably.

"Truthfully?" Her voice turned serious as she cautiously sipped the champagne. It was her first taste of alcohol since the fateful night of her arrival in Tucson.

"Well, I can't pretend the idea didn't cross my mind," he admitted slowly, a little roughly. "Knowing you're a woman who keeps her word, I suppose it's a temptation to keep trying to bind you with promises. But I would have married you, regardless of the wording in the marriage vows. I wanted you to know I was making a commitment to you, Emmy. I couldn't think of any other way to do it in this day and age. You never seemed to ask for promises from me, so I thought I'd give them to you in the form of a wedding service,'' he explained, sounding awkward all of a sudden.

''Oh, Julian,'' she whispered gently, touching the side of his face with her fingertips in a gesture of undisguised love. ''I never asked for promises because I've always known on some level that I could trust you.''

He caught her fingers in his hand, pulling her palm to his mouth and kissing her with exquisite intimacy on her wrist. ''And I think I've known from the first that I could trust you. Emmy, I love you so much!''

He moved his mouth to her lips in a kiss of promise that would span a lifetime.

''I love you, Julian.''

Unsteadily, Julian removed her glass from her hand and set it down beside his before turning back to place his palm on the curve of her breast. Emelina felt the tenderness and the urgency and the possession in his touch and her arms wound around his neck, pulling him to her. When she felt her nipple hardening beneath his palm and realized where the intimacy was leading, Emelina hesitated briefly.

''Julian, someone will see us!''

''No,'' he growled. ''No one can see into this corner of the garden, and if anyone dares come to the gate, Xerxes will scare him off.''

She relaxed with a moan of surrender as he fastened his mouth once more on hers. Slowly, with loving care they fed the passion between them. Emelina's clothing seemed to melt away from her body and somehow Julian's was quickly disposed of, too.

"I want you, wife," he muttered hoarsely as they lay naked together. His strong thigh touched hers, and he used one wide hand on her hips to draw her more firmly against him.

"And I want you, husband," Emelina breathed, glorying in the delicious sensations they produced so readily together. She moved her breasts gently against the cloud of curling hair on his chest and he groaned under the blatant provocation.

His hands moved over her with sure intimacy, rediscovering her with possessive satisfaction until Emelina was throbbing with the force of her desire. She touched him in turn, her fingertips sometimes gentle, sometimes wicked, but always loving.

Slowly they merged, coming closer and closer together on every level until, with an aching exclamation of need, Julian parted her legs with his hand and lowered himself into her pulsating warmth.

"Oh, God, Emmy," he grated as he filled her completely, losing himself in her even as he took possession. "Oh, my God!"

Together they rode out the gentle storm, each clinging to the other as if nothing in the universe could drive them apart, and when it was over, Julian continued to nestle into Emelina's welcoming embrace, his body never leaving hers.

"Do you know," he said in tones of wonder as he looked into her eyes, "that I never realized until I met you what this was all about?"

She smiled dreamily. "Sex?"

"No." He shook his head with grave certainty. "I knew what sex was all about. But I knew nothing of making love."

She saw the honesty in his eyes. "I understand, darling. It's the same for me. I never had an inkling about what it meant to really make love until I met you."

He grinned suddenly, his mood lightening as he regarded his charmingly tousled wife. "I would have thought a born romantic like you would have had it all figured out long ago. Surely with your vivid imagination?..."

"Imagination," Emelina declared firmly, "can only take a woman so far." She shifted beneath his heaviness, luxuriating in the way his body meshed so perfectly with hers. "Julian?"

"Hmmm?" He was beginning to nibble experimentally at the lobe of her ear.

"Have you decided how I'm going to pay off my debt?"

"Yes, I have, as a matter of fact." He raised his head, dark eyes laughing with love. "I will consider the debt paid the day you finally learn to make respectable coffee. I came to that decision only this morning when you handed me your latest attempt."

Emelina winced. "That could take me the rest of my life! You can be very hard to please when it comes to your coffee!"

He bent to her earlobe once more. "Umm. That's the whole idea. I'll have you in my clutches for the rest of your life." There was a husky note in his voice.

Emelina became aware of the tightening of his body, and her softness began to react to the distinct hardening of him within her. The warm tingling sensation seeped into her veins, becoming liquid fire. Emelina's eyes widened questioningly. "Julian?" she breathed.

"Don't worry, sweetheart," he murmured with deep urgency. "It's not a figment of your imagination." And he proceeded to illustrate the reality of his love.

* * * * *

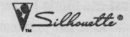

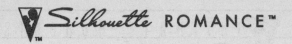